"What's wron... urgently as he... hurried her a... next street.

"Nothing. Everything." The heat sang up his arm while the spot on his back burned. "I have a—"

Feeling. Reid had meant to say. But the deafening *rat-tat-tat* of automatic gunfire drowned him out. This was it. The killer had caught up with Stephanie, and to hell with anyone else who got in the way.

Stephanie screamed and covered her ears. Reid yelled, "No!" and felt the anger blaze high. He pushed her into a shallow doorway off the alley and yanked his weapon clear. Wanting, needing to see the man who had done all this.

Wanting to make him suffer.

The hail of noise intensified and Reid heard screaming out in the street beyond. He tensed, wanting to go and help but needing to stay with Stephanie. To protect her.

Available in March 2005 from Silhouette Intrigue

Secret Witness
JESSICA ANDERSEN

*First published in Great Britain 2005
Silhouette Books, Eton House, 18-24 Paradise Road,
Richmond, Surrey TW9 1SR*

© Dr Jessica S Andersen 2004

ISBN 0 373 22762 0

46-0305

*Printed and bound in Spain
by Litografia Rosés S.A., Barcelona*

JESSICA ANDERSEN

Though she's tried out professions ranging from cleaning sea lion cages to cloning glaucoma genes, from patent law to training horses, Jessica is happiest when she's combining all these interests with her first love—writing. These days she's delighted to be writing full-time on a farm in rural Connecticut that she shares with a small menagerie of animals and a hero named Brian. She loves to hear from readers. You can write to her at PO Box 204, Voluntown, CT 06384, USA.

CAST OF CHARACTERS

Stephanie Alberts—An ex-husband and an ex-boyfriend have taught her to trust no one, but now she must rely on Detective Reid Peters to keep her daughter safe.

Reid Peters—The Boston detective doesn't believe there's any place in his life for soft emotions or a family. Will the danger to Stephanie and her child change his mind?

Jilly Alberts—Stephanie's daughter is nothing more than a pawn in a mad game of genetic chess. Or is she?

Detective Sturgeon—The veteran detective knows Reid better than anyone.

James Makepeace—The circumstantial evidence against the basement-dwelling handyman is strong.

Aunt Maureen—She would do anything to keep Stephanie and Jilly safe, but this time it might not be enough.

Derek Bott—His DNA was found at the scene of the crime, but his alibi is unbreakable.

Dwayne Bott—He will do anything to keep his brother out of jail. Anything.

For my critique partner, Liana Dalton, who
always knows when to say, "You can do better!"
and when to say, "Where's the rest?"

Chapter One

"Jilly? Jilly, where are you?" Stephanie Alberts launched herself up the stairs toward her daughter's bedroom. The starched white lab coat tangled around her calves. The nerves that had sizzled to life when Maureen had called her home from work clutched at her heart.

Not this, her mind begged. *Please not this.*

"Are you in here, baby?" she called into the frilly little room, trying to keep it light in case Jilly was only hiding. "Look! Mommy's home early. Don't you want to come out and play?"

There were no furtive, laughing eyes peering out from beneath the bed. No thumping of tiny feet running across the thick braided rug.

The little room was full of things—stuffed animals and model horses and the ruffled child-sized bed that Steph and Luis had picked out before Jilly was born. But there were no miniature red sneakers sticking out from beneath the frothy pink curtains. No stifled giggles.

"Jilly? Jilly, answer me or you're going to be in

big trouble!'' The sick feeling in Steph's stomach
was getting worse by the minute. Where was her
baby?

She felt a touch on her shoulder and whirled, hoping against hope—but it was only her aunt Maureen.

''She's not in the house. I told you, I looked ev-
erywhere. I'm sorry. I'm so sorry!'' The older
woman's gray eyes filled. Her soft cheeks trembled.
Even so many years ago, when she'd told the eight-
year-old Steph that her parents were dead, Maureen
hadn't looked this devastated.

The comparison was terrifying. Steph pushed it
aside. ''She has to be somewhere! If she's not in the
yard, then she's in the house.'' Her voice rose. She
couldn't help it. ''She *has* to be here! Jilly? Jilly,
you come out here right this minute!''

The doorbell rang and Steph glanced out the window. A blue-and-white cruiser was parked on the
cobblestones outside the narrow house, looking out
of place amidst carefully tended homes whose exte-
riors had barely changed since Paul Revere's ride.

''The police are here,'' she said on a note of rising
hysteria as the bell rang again. ''Why are they here?
Oh God, what if—?''

Maureen tugged her into the hall, down the stairs,
and Steph could feel the other woman's hand shaking, could hear the quiver in her voice when she said,
''I called them right after I called you. I swear to
you, Stephanie, that I didn't take my eyes off Jilly
for more than a moment. I think…''

Maureen couldn't finish.

Steph tried to force words between her numb lips, but they stuck as her aunt opened the door to reveal a pair of uniformed officers standing shoulder to shoulder. The bottom dropped out of her world as reality kicked in.

Jilly was gone.

WHEN HIS cell phone burbled a tinny version of Beethoven's Fifth, Reid balanced the weights on his chest, glared at the phone and lost count of his repetitions.

"Don't answer it," he told himself firmly. It was his first day off in over a month, for heaven's sake, and he'd planned on doing some serious relaxing.

He deserved it. The Solomon brothers were behind bars awaiting arraignment, and even District Attorney Hedlund had grudgingly agreed that Reid and his partner had built a solid case against the two punks. The owners of the robbed convenience stores had all agreed to testify, and Chinatown was safer by another two criminals. It was a done deal.

Da-da-da-*DUM*. The phone seemed to ring louder the longer he ignored it. He started to get that itchy feeling between his shoulder blades that he usually got just before a takedown went south. Or maybe it was just sweat running down his back and he was a paranoid cop who was always ready to assume the worst.

Da-Da-Da-*DUM*. "Damn it." He banged the free weights back onto their rack and snatched up the phone. "Peters."

There was no answer. In the background, he could hear the squawk of a radio and loud, urgent voices.

Reid snapped, "Sturgeon, is that you? What're you doing at the station? This is our first day off in forever, and—"

"Detective Peters?" The soft, tearful female voice was most definitely not that of Reid's partner, but it sounded familiar. His heart gained a beat and he angled the phone away from his ear for a belated glance at the display.

"Yes, this is Peters." His libido gave a big BA-BOOM when he saw the number and the name, but then the radio squealed again in the background and the itch intensified. "Miss Alberts? Stephanie? What's wrong?"

Loud silence again, then she gulped, clearly fighting a sob. "I'm sorry to bother you on your day off, but you gave me your card..." He was drawing breath to tell her it was fine and please get to the point when she hiccupped and said, "My daughter's gone."

Reid's stomach sank like a stone. He'd never met Stephanie's daughter, but his mind quickly supplied the image of another child, a broken body lying curled around a rag doll that was no more lifeless than the little girl. God, he hated it when there were kids involved.

"I'll be right there."

When he pulled up in front of Stephanie Alberts's house a few minutes later, Reid thought that the collection of cruisers and uniforms outside the lovely historic home seemed an abomination. Nothing bad should happen in a neighborhood where flags streamed from every front door and the Freedom Trail was a red stripe down the middle of the brick sidewalk on either side of the cobblestone road. Tasteful brass plaques gleamed beside doorways, engraved with the names of builders and dates and important moments in the American Revolution.

This was Patriot District. Nothing bad should happen in Patriot. It was a national landmark, for Chrissakes.

"I'm sorry, sir. You can't go up there." A uniform reached out to detain Reid and he yanked out his badge.

"Peters. Chinatown. And don't get in my way," he snarled.

Though they both knew he had zero jurisdiction, the rookie nodded him through.

Smart kid.

Peters saw Stephanie's aunt Maureen first. She grabbed him and ushered him to the back of the narrow house. He heard movement upstairs, and knew the Patriot District cops were doing their thing. The house felt like terror and tears, an all-too-familiar litany in Reid's world.

"I'm so glad you're here." There were stifled sobs in Maureen's eyes and voice, and the hand on his arm trembled. The two of them had met across Stephanie's hospital bed a year ago, and the older woman looked no less frantic now than she had when her niece had been brought to the hospital, badly beaten by a man Reid should've gotten to first. "I only took my eyes off Jilly for a moment. Not even that. More like a split second, and she was gone."

She ushered him to the back of the house, where Stephanie was sitting with pictures of a dark-haired child heaped in front of her on the kitchen table. In the most recent of the photos, the girl looked about three or four years old.

"We only need a couple," Officer Murphy from Patriot said, and the woman at the table nodded jerkily. The cut-glass light above the table shone down on her, picking out the russet highlights in her curly hair and placing her lowered face in soft shadow.

Not for the first time, Stephanie Alberts reminded Reid of the Renaissance paintings down at the Museum of Fine Art—all porcelain skin and delicate curves. He'd seen paintings like that when he was a boy, before the old man had found out about the art class and hit the roof.

Since then, there had been no time for art appreciation, and very little time for Reid to think of Stephanie Alberts.

But he had anyway.

"Of course. Silly of me." She stirred the photographs with her index finger.

"Steph? Detective Peters is here." Maureen tugged Reid into the room. Stephanie's head snapped up. Her eyes immediately filled with relief and more tears and Reid felt a rush of uncharacteristic emotion.

Especially uncharacteristic for a cop who'd been repeatedly turned down by the woman in question.

He wanted to pull her into his arms and tell her everything would be okay. He wanted to offer her his shoulder to cry on, and stroke her back until she was done. He wanted to hold her hand the way he'd done those four long days it had taken her to wake up in the hospital.

But he didn't. Instead, he looked away from the woman who'd told him in no uncertain terms that she didn't want to be involved with him, turned to Officer Murphy and said, "I know I don't belong here, but it's my day off. Cut me some slack and let me help. I'm a family friend."

Leanne Murphy's canny eyes cut from Peters to Stephanie and back again before she nodded. "We can use all the help we can get."

STEPH WASN'T SURE why it had seemed so imperative that she call Detective Peters. She barely knew the man. They'd met at her work, when the Watson lab at Boston General's Genetic Research Building had been the scene of several crimes.

Steph's boss, Dr. Genie Watson, had been brutally attacked in the lab darkroom. At first, it had seemed a random—though horrific—event, but a string of "accidents" and a car bombing had soon followed. Genie had been the target of a madman intent on protecting an inheritance he wasn't genetically heir to.

It had been during the investigation that Steph met Detective Peters. Even then, she'd been uncomfortable around the man. She'd just begun an intense relationship with a pharmaceutical rep named Roger, and it seemed disloyal for her to notice Peters's piercing eyes, broad shoulders and long, swinging strides. So she'd resisted the attraction and focused on Roger—and she'd nearly paid with her life when it turned out that her new boyfriend was using her to gain access to the lab.

One dark night, Roger had taken Steph's keycard, her self-respect, and nearly her life. Then he'd gone after his real target—Genie Watson.

Genie had survived, thanks to the protection—and love—of Dr. Nick Wellington, her former adversary. Now her husband. Steph had survived, too, though she'd been in the hospital for several weeks recovering from the beating.

Peters had been there, she remembered, sitting by her bedside, his eyes hooded with dark thoughts. Part of her had wanted to reach out to him, but she'd forced herself to turn away. Later, she'd refused his calls. He was a reminder of a time she'd rather forget. A near-fatal misjudgment that had proven again that she had abysmal taste in men and was better off alone.

She wasn't even sure why she'd kept his card, but it had leapt into her hand after the first wave of police questioning had finished and the officers had begun the search. When he'd arrived, for a moment, she'd felt as though everything was going to be okay. He'd see to it, though he didn't look quite like the Detective Peters she remembered.

She was used to seeing him in a suit and tie. Even

when he'd visited her in the hospital, he'd been wearing work clothes, with his tie loosened and his top button undone. But her call had interrupted his day off, and Stephanie realized something she'd only suspected before… Detective Reid Peters, handsome enough in a suit and tie, was downright devastating in casuals.

The jeans and cutoff sweatshirt didn't detract from the commanding impact of his wide shoulders or the military-straight posture that stretched him to a full six-three. The soft shirt clung to bulges and ridges that the suits had covered, and Steph wondered how she could have forgotten the striking contrast between his mid-brown crew cut and the light hazel, almost gold of his eyes.

Then she wondered how she could be thinking of such things when her daughter was missing.

Peters asked Officer Murphy, "How long has the girl been gone?"

Having noticed the female gleam that had entered Murphy's eye when Reid arrived, and hating herself for caring, Stephanie snapped, "Almost two hours. Maureen called me at two-ten and it's close to four now." The reality of it closed in and all thoughts of the handsome detective fled when Steph stared down at the photographs spread across her kitchen table. It was four. Jilly should be sitting there eating crackers and peanut butter. "She missed her snack."

Tears threatened again, and she cursed herself for all of it. Faintly, she heard Maureen sobbing in the living room and her head throbbed where the hairline crack had long since knit. She wished that once, just once, she had someone other than Aunt Maureen to lean on.

Sometimes they were barely enough to prop each other up.

There was a sudden commotion at the front of the house. Feet pounded on the upstairs floorboards and excited voices shouted outside. Officer Murphy grabbed the muted radio at her belt, turned up the volume, and barked a question. Steph couldn't understand the response, but she knew what the sudden tension in the room must mean.

For better or worse, they'd found Jilly.

Her stomach heaved and she tasted bile as a parade of macabre images flashed through her mind, courtesy of every forensics program she'd ever watched on TV. She tried to make her legs carry her outside. Tried to ask the question, but was afraid to because until someone said otherwise, she could believe that Jilly was okay.

She *had* to be okay. Steph didn't think she could bear it if anything happened to Jilly. The little girl was her lifeline. Her life. A perfect little person who'd been created by an imperfect union.

Steph felt Peters behind her, and drew an ounce of strength from his solid presence, which was more familiar and welcome than it should have been. He asked the question while her stomach tied itself up in knots.

"Is the girl okay?"

Steph might have found it odd that Peters hadn't

said Jilly's name once since he'd arrived, but that thought disappeared the instant Officer Murphy smiled. "They found her across the street in that little park. She's okay."

Thank God! was Steph's only thought as her feet carried her out the door to her daughter.

A SCANT HOUR later the Patriot cops were ready to pack it up and call it a day, but Reid wasn't so sure.

"Something about this just doesn't feel right," he insisted. "You're telling me that a three-and-a-half-year-old girl wanders across the street, down a half mile of paths, and nobody sees her? Then two hours later, a jogger tells Officer Dunphy he saw a little girl over by the duck pond, and *boom!* There she is? Where was she the rest of the time? And where's the jogger?"

"We have his name and number," Officer Murphy replied, irritated. "And it's not unheard of for a young child to follow, say, a puppy and end up lost. Jilly is home, and the paramedics said there's absolutely no evidence of anything being…done to her. We're canvassing the neighborhood to see if anyone saw something suspicious, and beyond that it's a closed case. Why don't you go…console Miss Alberts rather than trying to make my job harder than it has to be?"

Reid glared, but couldn't completely fault Murphy. She had a point, there was zero evidence that Stephanie's daughter had been the victim of anything more than a lapse in babysitting on her great-aunt's part. And she was also right that he was there strictly as Stephanie's friend, not as a cop.

Speaking of which…he should probably be going. Crisis over. Time to get on with his day off.

He scratched at the low-grade itch between his shoulder blades and nodded curtly when Murphy excused herself. He glanced into the living room, feeling as though his eyes were being forced there by a magnetic pull. Mother and daughter were wrapped around each other on the couch, and it tugged at his heart to see Steph's soft red curls clutched in the little girl's fist. The kid was awake and seemed content to snuggle in her mother's lap.

Reid couldn't blame her. And boy, did he need to get out of here.

He didn't do the kid thing. He did the casual thing.

But the bad feeling he just couldn't shake compelled him to ask Stephanie, "Are you sure she won't answer a few simple questions, even if you ask them?" It seemed to him that three and a half was plenty old enough for some gentle interrogation, even if Officer Don't-Make-My-Day-Longer-You-Schmuck Murphy thought there was no reason for it.

But Stephanie shook her head. "Jilly's a little shy. She doesn't talk much. We're working on it." She dropped a kiss on her daughter's dark hair, and Reid found himself wondering about the little girl's father.

Again, he thought of paintings. He hadn't been to the MFA in fifteen years and hadn't painted in longer, but Stephanie Alberts made him think of art.

So did her daughter. While Stephanie could have been the model for Botticelli's misty, ethereal *Birth of Venus*—before Venus got fat—her daughter had stepped straight out of the Spanish works of the next century. She was a study in sharp angles and warm, dark eyes.

"What about her father?" He hadn't meant to ask, but once the question was out there, Reid consoled himself with the thought that it was a logical next step. More often than not, kids were snatched by family members.

"Luis? What about him?"

"Would he take her?"

Stephanie clutched her daughter until the child squirmed a protest. "She wasn't taken. She wasn't. She just wandered off." But Reid could see the doubts in her big blue-green eyes. Or were those his doubts? "And besides, Luis is...Luis couldn't have taken her."

"Detective? The others are leaving now." At Maureen's gesture, Reid joined her at the front door. They bade goodbye to the last of the Patriot District cops.

When he was alone with the older woman, Reid said, "Stephanie's daughter doesn't talk at all?"

Though they hadn't kept in touch, he and Maureen had become friends of a sort while they had both watched over Stephanie's bed at the hospital. The older woman nodded. "That's right. We keep hoping she'll start speaking again, but..." She shrugged. "Not yet."

Reid glanced back toward the living room. "It would help if she could tell us what happened today."

Maureen's gray eyes sharpened. "You don't think she just wandered?"

He shrugged. "There's nothing to say any different. I just like to be thorough, that's all." Not wanting to dwell on his unfounded suspicions, Reid changed the subject. "Have you taken her to any specialists? Do you know why she's…quiet?"

He didn't really want to know about the kid, he assured himself. He didn't do kids. He was just gathering all the information he could. Then he'd be on his way home.

"Her father left when she was about a year old," Maureen supplied after a quick glance into the other room. "It was…messy. Jilly had just begun talking, but shut down after that. The doctors said not to worry, she'd sing when she was ready. She'd just started to come out of her shell last fall…"

She trailed off and Reid nodded. "And then Steph was attacked."

"Yes. We didn't tell Jilly what had happened, of course, but children know things. She's been extremely shy ever since. Steph has been talking recently about more therapy, but Jilly hated it so much before that we're afraid of making things worse." Maureen shrugged. "And then this…? I don't know what happens now."

Reid touched Maureen's shoulder. "She's home.

That's what matters, right? Leave the rest of it to the police—it's our job.''

Like it had been their job to arrest small-time drug dealer Alfonse Martinez six months ago, never dreaming that the ensuing firefight would take the life of a three-year-old girl who wasn't supposed to be in the house in the first place. A little girl who looked an awful lot like Stephanie's daughter.

He really needed to get out of here.

Reid touched Maureen's shoulder again, then took himself back into the living room to say goodbye, standing far away from the pretty, domestic scene on the couch. If his own father hadn't been enough to convince Reid that cops have no business around small children, the memory of that little girl curled around a blood-soaked rag doll had driven the point home.

There was no way to mix a badge with family.

And since Stephanie was a mother and Reid was a cop…well, he was just lucky she'd turned him down last year when he'd let lust overrun his good sense and asked her out. Twice.

Lucky. Yeah, that was it.

She lifted her head from her daughter's hair and gave him a watery smile. The kid had dropped off to sleep with one thumb in her mouth and her other hand clutching her mother's hair. Steph stood, balancing the little girl easily on one hip. ''Follow me up? I want to put her down for a nap, then maybe you'll join me in a cup of coffee.''

Reid felt a tightness in his chest, a strange tug of

war. Then he took a step away and held up an impersonal hand. "Thanks for the offer, but I'm going to take off. Everything seems okay here."

"Oh." The warmth in her jade-green eyes faded a little, the corners of her wide, generous mouth turned down at the edges, and the misty radiance around her dimmed a bit. "I'm sorry, I thought... never mind." Her mouth turned up again and she held out her free hand to him. "Then thank you so much for all your help. I'm sorry to have interrupted your day off."

He took her hand and felt as though he ought to kiss it. Suckle her fingers one by one.

Hit himself over the head with a brick until sanity returned.

He gave the dainty hand a brisk shake instead. "That's my job, Miss Alberts. I'm just glad your daughter is back safe and sound. I...I guess I'll see you around." And he escaped out onto the cobbled street with barely a goodbye for Maureen.

Once he was outside and felt that he could fill his lungs for the first time in hours, Reid sucked in a deep breath and took a casual look around the neighborhood while he waited for his heartbeat to return to normal.

He thought about the free weights back at his place near the Chinatown station house. Thought about the frozen pizza he'd planned for his dinner, and about the Red Sox game that was scheduled to start in an hour. Thought about She Devil, the enormously pregnant stray cat that had adopted him a few weeks ago and just that morning had started building a nest in his underwear drawer.

He thought about his day off.

And headed for the park where Jilly Alberts had been found.

"WELL, I GUESS I read *that* wrong," Steph murmured to her sleeping daughter as she climbed the stairs, then put Detective Peters and his incredible…intellect out of her mind. Mostly. Tonight was for Jilly, not for sexy detectives in cutoff sweatshirts, or for a moment of forgetting that she'd sworn off men for good.

She paused in the doorway, thinking of how panicked she'd been standing in her daughter's bedroom just hours ago. She could hardly believe that the horror had ended in hours rather than the days that seemed to have elapsed between Aunt Maureen's call to the genetics lab and the police finding Jilly unharmed in the park.

Her daughter had simply wandered away. She hadn't been kidnapped. Hadn't been hurt.

Steph tucked Jilly into bed and the little girl didn't make a sound as she curled on her side and wrapped one thin arm around her favorite stuffed bear. Steph kissed her daughter's forehead and brushed the dark hair smooth. "Don't ever scare me like that again, okay, baby? I don't think my heart can take it."

Leaving the door ajar and the light on in the hall as she hadn't done in months, she padded back downstairs, meeting her aunt in the hallway. Maureen was carrying a pair of mugs. Offering Steph the one with a cartoon cat dangling from a tree branch and the caption Hang in There, Maureen said, "Thought we could both use some hot chocolate."

Hot chocolate in the middle of the summer. It had seemed an odd idea to Steph when she'd first come to live with Aunt Maureen after the car crash that had killed her parents, but over the years she'd realized it was Maureen's best answer for things she didn't know how to fix.

Steph had downed gallons of the frothy liquid in those first few months.

"Bless you." She took the mug and they both collapsed on the couch. Steph sipped, coughed and grinned as the liqueur kicked at her chest. "Hot chocolate, hot toddy, same thing." She closed her eyes. "You were a rock today, Aunt Maureen. I can't thank you enough."

Maureen shook her head. "Don't thank me. If I'd been paying better attention, this never would have happened. I was watching her and that man next door was making an awful racket on that horn of his. I turned my head for an instant to demand that he have some respect for the sanctity of our neighborhood, and when I looked back…she was gone."

Aunt Maureen's eyes welled up at the memory, and her lower lip began to tremble. Then, as if her words had conjured it, there was a wail from outside. The eerie noise shivered up several octaves, then ran back down like water, leaving the hairs standing up on the back of Steph's neck.

She had a quick vision of the lost souls of the Revolutionary War calling to each other across the cobbled streets.

The sound rose again, eerie and sad, and Maureen swore, tears forgotten in the face of her long-pitched battle with their neighbor. "That man! Has he no sense of decency?"

She launched herself from the couch and stomped for the front door, seeming not to notice that the banshee screech had resolved itself to a glissando of sweet, sexy saxophone.

The door banged open and Steph heard her aunt bellow, "Mortimer, you dog, I'll sue you for noise pollution, see if I don't! Cut that out!"

Her words were answered by what sounded like a Bronx cheer à la saxophone, and the door slammed shut behind Maureen, muting both the sax and the yelling. Steph didn't bother to run upstairs and close Jilly's door, knowing that her daughter could sleep through anything—

Including the digital ring of the telephone.

Steph picked up the handset and glanced at the display, which read Out of Area. It should've read No Number Listed Because I Pay To Negate Your Caller ID. She sighed. Some pieces of technology were downright useless.

She punched Talk. "Hello?"

Silence. A dead, heavy, pregnant silence. Then breathing.

Steph rolled her eyes. "If you're trying to scare

me, you'll have to do better than that, buster. I walk through the Combat Zone on the way to work.''

There was a chuckle. Then a harsh, oily voice. "I know how you walk to work, bitch. I also know where your pretty little girl went today, and it wasn't the park. Have I scared you yet?''

Scared wasn't the word for it. Not even close.

Terror, pure and clean, knifed through her like a scalpel and left her bleeding fear. She sucked in a breath, heard her aunt and Mortimer arguing outside and felt as if she was drowning.

She could almost *feel* the person on the other end of the line smile. "Thought that might get your attention. Here's the deal. Today was a warning. I have a little job for you. If you do it, you and your family will be safe. If you don't, or if you tell anyone about this, you'll get the little girl back in pieces next time. Or I'll do the old woman. Or both. Do you understand?''

Her whole body shaking, Steph could only nod into the phone. When he continued to wait, she tried to speak through her suddenly parched mouth and managed a whispered, "I understand.''

There was a satisfied silence, then a murmur in the background. The voice returned. "Oh yeah, and no cops or both the kid and the old woman are dead. Understand?''

Steph could feel the walls of the cage slide into place around her. Felt the fear bleed through to drip on the floor. She managed, "I understand," and felt the numbness spread up her fingers to her heart. ''What do you want me to do?''

The voice turned hard. Implacable. ''Make sure the Makepeace DNA is a positive match. Or else.''

Chapter Two

The next morning, Stephanie awoke feeling as though she'd slept in a bed that was three sizes too small for her. When she glanced around at the animals and ruffles and felt the small, hot bump of her daughter beside her, she realized that was exactly what she'd done.

Then she remembered the rest of it and her stomach clenched like a fist.

"God!" She jolted in the bed and her hands flew to Jilly, grabbing up the sleepy girl and making sure she was really there.

Another child might have yelled in protest, but not this one. She just looked up at Steph with wide, worried eyes as if to say, What's wrong this time? She'd lived through so much already—Luis's rages, Steph's tears, her time in the hospital after Roger...

What's wrong *this* time? Jilly's eyes asked, and Steph might have laughed, but she was afraid it would come out a scream, because *everything* was wrong.

Send her back to you in pieces, the dead dark

voice whispered at the edge of her mind and it wasn't until Jilly started to squirm that Steph realized she was clutching her daughter even tighter, as though a mother's arms would be enough protection.

At the thought of protection, her mind jumped immediately to the sight of Detective Peters lounging in her kitchen doorway the day before, bulging arms crossed over the wide chest of the cutoff sweatshirt. Snug, faded denim and a gun tucked at the small of his back. Amber, knowing eyes that had changed when they'd looked at the child.

No cops or both the kid and the old woman are dead. No. She couldn't call him. She'd been warned and she'd learned her lesson about trusting men. She was on her own, and the only way to be sure of Jilly's safety was for her to go to work and run the experiment. The voice had said so.

The Makepeace samples were already prepared, taken from the rape kit Detective Sturgeon had delivered a week ago. She'd seen it in the papers, though she tried not to read anything about the lab cases she handled for the police. The headline had jolted her, Suspect Charged in Chinatown Child Rape, and she'd read several paragraphs of lurid details before realizing that the rapist's DNA was sitting in her lab fridge.

Now she wondered.

Make sure the Makepeace DNA is a positive match. Or else. Did the voice have reason to believe it wouldn't be a match? Did he know for sure that Makepeace hadn't done it? Because he had raped the little girl himself? If so, that was even more reason to protect Jilly any way she could. Steph shivered in the warm air of a summer morning. She saw a yawning chasm opening up in front of her, a choice she'd never thought to make.

If the DNA matched, Jilly and Maureen were safe. If it didn't...

The alternative was unthinkable. Therefore, there was only one solution.

The DNA would match. She'd make sure of it.

DOWN THE STREET from Boston General Hospital, Sturgeon's voice cut across the usual din of the Chinatown Station. "Hi, honey. I'm home!"

Reid let his feet slide off the edge of the desk and thump to the floor while he glared his partner. "Go suck on a peppermint, Sturgeon," he said, but he didn't really mean it.

Fifty-something, jowly and slightly pop-eyed, Reid's partner bore an unfortunate resemblance to his animal namesake. He was also one of the sharpest men in Chinatown, and Reid had been honored when the veteran detective had partnered him seven years earlier.

Sturgeon pulled one of the candies from the breast pocket of his already-rumpled suit and held it out. At Peters's headshake, he shrugged, unwrapped the pinwheel with a deft one-handed flick, and popped it in his mouth.

"You have a good day off?" he asked around the peppermint.

Reid shrugged. "It was fine. You?" He didn't need to ask. If it'd been a lousy day, Sturgeon would be crunching the candy with a vengeance. The rate at which he devoured mints was a pretty good barometer of his mood.

"Took Jennie and the grandkids to that water park in New Hampshire. They've got this great new slide that shoots you down the hill almost in freefall." Sturgeon's eyes took on a faraway, happy look. "The kids loved it, and while we were standing in line this pretty blonde lost her bikini top on the way down." He grinned. "Jen tried to act mad that I looked, but later that night she gave me this reenactment..." Sturgeon trailed off and Reid held up a hand.

"Enough! No more, please. I'm begging you!"

He imagined Sturgeon in swimming trunks, surrounded by his three grandkids and grinned. Tried not to imagine Sturgeon and his trim, zippy wife engaged in a game of "Oops, I lost my bikini top!" and failed.

Tried to imagine himself taking children and a wife to a water park and scowled.

Sturgeon chuckled and hitched himself onto the corner of Reid's desk. "You wouldn't be begging me if you had a wife of your own, you know."

Reid rolled his eyes. "Don't start."

It was beyond him how Sturgeon had managed to stay married thirty years and counting. He was the guy who threw the curve on cop demographics—the one half of one percent that was happily married.

The noise level started to rise as the shift changed.

Sturgeon didn't bother to lower his voice and a passing rookie snickered when the detective said, "I mean, what's the problem here? You're healthy, employed, only mildly lazy, and although I don't really see it, Jennie tells me that you're H-O-T hot. Apparently, your ass is exquisite."

There was a guffaw from three desks over. Reid glared, but couldn't tell which of his so-called friends it had been.

"I don't," he said in measured tones, "want to talk about your wife's opinion of my ass." Though he was flattered in a sick sort of way. "I don't want to talk about my sex life." Or lack thereof. He hadn't dated steadily since he'd accidentally yelled the wrong woman's name in the throes and had been summarily dumped on his head. When he'd gone to find the witness whose name he *had* yelled, he'd arrived at her house only to learn she'd been put in the hospital by a man who'd been on his list of suspects to question the next day.

He hadn't yet forgiven himself for that one. Nor had he quite escaped the feeling that there was something not quite right about her kid's reappearance the day before.

"And…" He pushed the thought aside and pointed at his partner. "I most certainly don't want to talk about *your* sex life."

Unperturbed, Sturgeon unwrapped another mint and popped it home. He shrugged. "Then what do you want to talk about? You gonna tell me what's bugging you, and why there're enough coffee cups on the desk to prove you spent the night here on your first day off in over a month?''

Reid scowled at the telltale cups. ''I was working.''

''On what? There's nothing on our desks except some leftover paperwork and old coffee cups. Don't tell me you came in to do paperwork—that's really sick. And don't tell me you like the coffee.''

''Stephanie Alberts's kid was snatched yesterday.''

Sturgeon inhaled his mint. ''Come again?''

''Remember Stephanie Alberts? Redheaded lab tech from last year's trouble over at Boston General?''

Sturgeon nodded and sketched a set of curves in the air to indicate that he remembered her. She was hard to forget, and both of them had been burned by that case when her boyfriend—who was barely even a suspect—had beaten her into a coma.

There had been a police detail outside the house where she was attacked and it hadn't made a damn bit of difference. She'd still ended up in Boston General, hooked to more machines than Reid had ever seen.

''Yeah, I remember her. The daughter was snatched? Why didn't you call me?''

Reid shrugged. ''It was over quick enough. Uniforms from Patriot District found the girl across the street in a park.''

''Then she just wandered off, right? No snatch.''

''Looks that way,'' Reid answered.

"But you don't think so."

Sturgeon knew him well. Reid nodded. "It doesn't feel right. The kid was gone for a couple of hours and the aunt swears she checked the park right away when she disappeared. Kid's not even four, so she couldn't have gotten very far in any case…"

"You ask Jilly?"

Reid was surprised that Sturgeon remembered the little girl's name when he hadn't. But then again, Sturgeon had kids of his own. It was probably in the daddy manual that you had to remember other kids' names.

Too bad Reid's old man hadn't read that particular owner's manual. Reid shook his head. "Kid doesn't talk."

Sturgeon frowned. "No?"

"The doctors say she'll talk when she's ready. The aunt made it sound like the parents' marriage ended badly and slowed her down." Reid wondered what *messy* meant. He hoped it hadn't been abuse, though he'd seen enough of it over the years. "She was just starting to talk when Steph was hospitalized last year."

"Steph?" Sturgeon wrinkled an eyebrow.

"Ms. Alberts. Anyway, questioning the kid was out, and Murphy over at Patriot didn't think much of my suspicions."

"Leanne Murphy is a good cop," Sturgeon commented, and Reid heard the subtext—*If she doesn't think there's anything suspicious, she's probably right.*

Reid shrugged. "So I took a walk around the park. Talked to a few neighbors." And had gotten more information about Steph's ex than he had about her daughter's disappearance.

He'd checked. Luis Monterro was still in prison on an embezzlement conviction. But the itch between his shoulder blades hadn't gone away.

"Any evidence of a snatch?" Sturgeon asked, "Or are you just looking for an excuse to sniff around a lady who's already turned you down twice?"

"I don't sniff." The only reason Sturgeon got away with comments like that was that he was a good partner and friend. Otherwise, Reid would've shot him a long time ago. "And no, there's no evidence she was kidnapped."

"Then let's get to work." Still perched on Reid's desk, Sturgeon reached over to his own and snagged a pile of torn notebook paper. He shuffled through. "Let's see—we have cleanup work on those two Santos punks, mostly paperwork." He tossed the scrap back on his desk. "A visit with D.A. Hedlund, and a lab run for the last batch of results."

Reid snagged the last piece of paper from Sturgeon's hand and tucked it into his own neat notebook. "I'll take the lab, you deal with Hedlund."

"Fine." Sturgeon cut him a glance and grinned. "And say hi to her for me, will you?"

Reid scowled and straightened his tie.

THE WALLS were watching her. She was sure of it. She could feel him out there, somewhere, watching to make sure she didn't make a mistake. Or was he watching the house instead? That was an even more terrifying thought. Though she'd insisted that Maureen keep Jilly inside for the day, he knew where they lived. How she walked to work.

He knew.

Stephanie glanced down at the blue latex-encased hands working their way through a plate of samples, and wondered whether they were still attached to her body. She hadn't consciously told them to set up the experiment, but they seemed to be doing fine without her.

What was she going to do? She looked quickly around the lab for the zillionth time, half expecting to find a stranger standing over by the ultra-low temp freezer, watching her. But there was nobody there.

Molly was at her bench working on the last few experiments they'd need to finish before they announced the discovery of the Fenton's Ataxia gene—a coup for their boss Genie Watson, whose best friend had died of the disease.

Terry was at the computer, his Adam's apple bobbing now and again as he struggled with the last part of his dissertation. Though a laboratory genius, Terry was a disaster at putting things into words. Normally, Steph would've been at the computer with him, helping make the science into language. But today she was frozen at her bench, afraid that the watcher would interpret the least social contact as betrayal.

I'll send her back in pieces.

She glanced out past the reception area, to where

the lab leaders' offices were dark. Genie and Nick were at a two-week genetics conference in Hawaii. Steph wished they were around. After everything they'd been through the year before, which had culminated with Nick subduing the murderous madman, Steph thought they would know what to do.

But then again, the lab leaders would probably insist on going to the police, and that wasn't an option.

There was no way Steph was endangering her child or her aunt by making yet another catastrophic error in judgment. She was going this one alone. She had no choice.

Beep-beep…beep-beep…beep-beep.

She glanced at her lab timer, a sophisticated clock that allowed her to monitor up to ten different experiments at once. Today, there was only one display in action, and it was blinking 00:00.

The Makepeace film was ready for processing.

Glancing around one more time, still convinced that she was being watched, Steph collected the freezer cassette from the counter where she'd let it defrost. *Be a match,* she prayed, though she feared it wasn't.

Normally, DNA gels didn't need to be frozen down with their films, but since one of the samples in this experiment had been badly degraded seminal fluid from the little girl's rape kit, Steph had needed to intensify the radioactive signal before she could see the results. Freezing the trapped radioactivity at minus eighty slowed the particles down long enough for them to bounce off a reflective screen and pass through the X-ray film a second time, effectively doubling the signal.

Ignoring the bite of cold metal through the thin latex gloves, Steph lugged the lightproof film cassette to the developer room and tried not to look back over her shoulder as she stepped into the hall.

Last year, Genie had been attacked inside the black, close room. She'd been badly beaten and left for dead. Though the space had been cleaned and repainted since, going through the revolving door and hearing it *rubba-thump* behind her still gave Steph the willies, particularly today.

What if *he* came in while she was developing the film? She'd be trapped.

The light lock gaped at her like a screaming black mouth, and she stepped into it on unsteady legs and let it roll shut behind her. When nothing sprang out of the darkness to grab her, she processed the clammy film as quickly as possible and escaped back into the lighted hallway. She snatched the processed X-ray film from the delivery port before it was completely dry.

And cursed sharply. Hopelessly.

At the other end of the hall, one of the techs looked up at her oath. "Everything okay, Steph?"

"Sure, Jared. Everything's fine," she answered automatically as her brain raced.

Make sure the Makepeace DNA is a positive match.

"Everything's fine," she repeated to herself just in case saying it made it true.

But it wasn't fine.

The Makepeace DNA wasn't a match.

What the hell was she going to do now?

REID PAUSED in the elevator lobby of the thirteenth floor and buzzed to be let in. He remembered the first time he'd seen Boston General's Genetic Research Building, and the big, hulking machines and the crisp, white-coated people that moved among them. It looked like something out of one of the science-fiction movies he'd watched as a kid when there wasn't a cops-and-robbers flick playing.

But this wasn't science fiction. It was real. And in the nine months the Chinatown station had been subcontracting its DNA forensics out to the Watson/Wellington lab, their conviction rate had risen ten percent.

Even D.A. Hedlund was grudgingly impressed.

The door swung open automatically as someone buzzed him in from within the maze of corridors that wound through the thirteenth floor. And as he turned toward the Watson side of the labyrinth, Reid remembered the day he and Sturgeon had been called out for an assault and attempted rape on this very floor.

Reid had been moved by the white-coated woman covered in blood and crumpled beneath a stainless-steel sink. He had been glad to see that Genie Watson was breathing and almost conscious when they carried her out of the tiny room on a stretcher. He had been annoyed at the number of feet that had tracked the blood evidence around the room, and he had been dreading the phone call he would have to make, canceling yet another date with Yvette. But then again, she'd been getting clingy. Making noises about commitment and—gulp—kids. He remembered thinking that maybe it wasn't a bad thing he was canceling on her again. He'd pushed his way out of the developer room, turned toward a knot of murmuring white-coated technicians to begin the necessary round of questioning—and felt like he'd been shot point-blank in the chest while wearing a Kevlar vest.

She was so tiny the lab coat swallowed her up and didn't even hint at her figure. Her curly red hair was so vivid that it had looked out of place against all that sterile white, and her wide, worried eyes had looked like wet jade.

Suddenly Yvette's five-foot-ten seemed gargantuan, her expensive hair too blond and her clothing too tight and colorful. He hadn't had the heart to tell Yvette about his waning desire for her, but she'd figured it out soon enough.

"Detective Peters?"

And there she was again. Dressed in a lab coat.

He looked around. Somehow, his feet had brought him to Stephanie's bench. She was standing, staring up at him with a sheaf of printouts clutched to her chest. The pages crinkled as her fingers tightened on them. They were already badly wrinkled, which was unusual for the military precision of the Watson lab.

"Can I help you, Detective Peters? If not, I'm quite busy. I have work to catch up on from yesterday.'' Though not quite rude, her tone certainly wasn't friendly. Tension seemed to emanate from her in waves, and as he watched, her eyes slid to a shadowy corner of the lab.

A tickle traveled across his left shoulder blade.

Seeming convinced there was nothing in the shadows, she brushed past him. The starched white cotton of her lab coat feathered across the back of his hand, leaving a hot wave of arousal in its wake and reminding him that about a year ago he'd developed a thing for lab coats. For redheads wearing lab coats and nothing else…

Test results, he reminded himself, *you're here for test results.* Then, when he took in the tense set of her shoulders and the nervous darting of her eyes, his reasons for being there suddenly seemed less important than they had a moment ago. The tingle centered on his spine.

Something was up.

''How's your daughter?'' he asked casually. ''Any ill effects from her field trip yesterday?''

She flinched, as though fearing he knew something she didn't, then shook her head. ''Um, no. She seems fine. In fact, I think she's come through this better than either Maureen or I. I'm still a basket case though, thinking of what might have happened, and if Maureen even lets her step foot outside the house today I'll be surprised.''

There was a quick tremble in her voice, and she fiddled with a mechanical pencil as she spoke, clicking the lead and then tapping the point on the hard lab bench until the fragile graphite snapped. Reid wondered whether that was all there was to it. Left-over nerves? Or something more?

He didn't have much experience with kids, but he'd heard the fierceness in Sturgeon's voice once or twice when one of the guppies had been threatened in very minor ways. Stephanie had been so deter-minedly tough the day before he supposed she might be suffering the backlash.

But if she looked over into the darkness next to that big machine one more time…

"Are you okay?" he asked, jerking his head at the corner. "You seem nervous."

She shook her head in quick denial. "No—not nervous. I'm fine. Everything's fine."

He nodded slowly, not believing her for a second but still not sure whether her daughter's disappear-ance had freaked her out or there was something else. "Okay, then." He paused. Clearly today wasn't a good day to ask her out for lunch. Then again, Reid thought, *never* would be a better time to ask her out—she had a kid, and Sturgeon's success aside, no kid needed a cop around.

So he shrugged, pushed aside the image of her wearing a lab coat, a pair of red high heels and noth-ing else, and said, "I need to pick up the latest DNA results for Sturgeon's and my cases. That'd be Make-peace, Garcia and Roberts." He knew it was careless of them to name their DNAs rather than numbering them so the results were blinded for the researchers, but really, what interest did a lab tech have in messing with police work?

She shook her head and clutched the papers tighter to her chest. "They're not ready yet."

That was not the answer he'd been looking for. "Not ready? What do you mean, not ready?" They needed those results for court dates, damn it. "Sturgeon got a message on his voice mail that they'd be finished this morning. Something go wrong?"

The itch intensified.

Stephanie shook her head. "You can have Garcia and Roberts, they're all set." She gestured at a pair of folders on her desk labeled with the names. "But the other isn't finished yet."

An empty folder labeled Makepeace lay open on the desk. "What happened to it? Is there something wrong with the sample?" Please don't let anything be wrong with the sample, he thought. D.A. Hedlund would have a cow and shifty, scummy Makepeace would walk on the one rape they'd managed to pin on him, out of a series of six.

Though the links between the ex-con handyman and little Mae Wong's rape were largely circumstantial, they'd been enough to arrest him and warrant the DNA sample. All they needed to get a conviction was a DNA match...but they *needed* that match. The case was a no-go without it.

"Sorry," she said, not looking sorry at all. "Technical difficulties. There was a problem with the thermocycling temperature, so the DNA didn't amplify correctly and I couldn't finish the test. I'll rerun the experiment today and have the results later in the week, okay?''

No, damn it. It wasn't okay. Reid didn't like the look in her eye, and he didn't like that the test wasn't done.

''Steph?'' Another tech's voice interrupted, ''Genie's on the phone for you. She wants to talk about the last batch of sequencing.''

Steph glanced from the lab phone and back to Reid, scowling as though she wished he would disappear. When he didn't, she made an irritated noise and stalked over to talk to her boss.

Reid couldn't have asked for better timing. He'd have to thank Dr. Watson the next time he saw her...once he asked her what the hell was going on in her lab. After making sure Steph was busy on the phone and had her back to him, he shuffled through the two finished folders she'd given him. The proper paperwork was there—along with the computer printout of the scanned film results and the calculated probabilities for and against DNA matches. They were both matches, thank God. Reid only hoped they went three for three.

He looked at the Makepeace folder again. It was still empty. No paperwork, no printout.

What had she been crumpling against her lab coat? Makepeace's results?

Reid shifted a few papers on her desk and uncovered an X-ray film of the type Genie Watson had once tried to explain to him. One side was labeled Makepeace, the other side Rape Kit Sample, along with a bunch of other stuff, labeled Ladder and CEPH and a few he couldn't even read.

"Couldn't finish the experiment, eh?" Reid murmured as he slid the film onto a flat lightbox and clicked it on the way Genie had shown him. The gray plastic sprang to life and he saw two rows of dark lines marching down the length of the film like grocery-store bar codes.

We test thirteen highly variable sites within the human genome, he remembered Genie explaining the DNA tests that could free or condemn a criminal with nothing more than a shadow of a bloodstain. *Through chance, it's possible that two people share the same size marker on one or both of their chromosomes. But the likelihood of two people—unless they're identical twins—being the same at every one of those thirteen markers is so low as to be nonexistent.* She had paused, then grinned. "Unless you were on the O.J. jury—in which case that point-zero-nine-percent of a chance is enough to cast doubt."

Reid remembered chuckling at the joke. But he wasn't chuckling now. Even to his untrained eye, it was clear that the Makepeace side and the rape kit side of the film didn't even come close to matching.

"Damn it." He and Sturgeon had been so sure James Makepeace had abducted little Mae Wong, raped her and left her for dead in a Dumpster down by the Science Museum. She'd lived—barely—but she would never be the same laughing, happy child Reid had seen in the pictures pressed on him by Mrs. Wong. The detectives had been fiercely glad to pin the crime on Makepeace, a slimy, basement-dwelling handyman who had access to the Wong home, priors for assault and sexual misconduct, and no alibi.

This had been the first of the rapes with DNA left behind, and the first involving a child. Though the break in pattern had bothered Reid, there were enough similarities that he and Sturgeon had hoped to nail down the one case and build up the others. They had done their jobs and come up with Makepeace.

Though he'd howled his innocence to anyone who'd listen, the wriggly piece of excrement had been held on Reid and Sturgeon's say-so—and lack of bail money—pending the DNA results and a trial.

They'd been so sure of him. Even the D.A. liked the Wong case. But it wasn't Makepeace's genetic material that had been taken from the little girl's torn body. He hadn't done it. Reid dropped the film back on Stephanie's desk and swore viciously, helplessly, knowing that it wasn't enough.

They didn't have their man.

"Sorry about that," Steph said, returning to her bench. "The day Nick and Genie left for a conference in Hawaii, we had a breakthrough in the Fenton's Ataxia project. We convinced her not to fly home, but..." She trailed off when she glanced at his face. Shrugged. "But you're not interested in that, are you? You're here for your results." She tapped the two files. "Here they are. I'll have the Makepeace results for you by the end of the week.

Sorry for the delay.'' Her voice didn't tremble as she lied straight to his face.

Reid felt his fist clench and wanted to hit something. This was a *child* they were talking about.

"No problem," he lied right back. "I'll catch you later in the week. Thanks for these." He lifted the finished folders in farewell and retraced his steps through the thirteenth floor to the elevator. He gritted his teeth and stabbed the elevator call button.

He didn't know what was going on, but he was sure as hell going to find out. And if Stephanie Alberts was screwing with his evidence, she'd be sorry.

Very, very sorry.

Chapter Three

Steph was alone in the lab that night, just shutting down the last of the big machines, when the phone rang. The sound shattered the humming silence like a scream.

"Damn!" She put a hand to her thumping heart and stared at the instrument as it rang a second time. She imagined a dead-sounding whisper, a snarl of accusation because she'd talked to a cop. A chuckle as he told her Jilly was gone.

The phone rang again. "It's not him," she told herself. "Just pick it up."

But she couldn't. Her feet were frozen in place, and she felt a sudden surge of the nausea that had been building ever since she'd looked into Detective Peters's gorgeous golden-brown eyes and lied her ass off.

She'd lied to a cop about an investigation. She was going to hell—or jail, whichever came first.

If the voice didn't get her before then.

The phone rang a third, fourth and fifth time as

she stared at it. Then it stopped. The answering machine did not click on.

He'd hung up.

Steph felt a massive shudder crawl down her back and she fled through the lab, slapping at switches and grabbing her purse almost as an afterthought. She was halfway to the elevator when she remembered.

I know how you walk to work, bitch.

The phone began to ring again. She shoved at the door to the elevator lobby and caromed into the little space, frantic to be away from the ringing phone and the voice in her head. Frantic to get to her daughter. She punched her security code into the door lock with trembling fingers and turned to jab at the elevator call button.

The car was already moving up toward the thirteenth floor.

He's coming, she thought hysterically, *he knows I didn't tell Detective Peters that the Makepeace DNA was a match. He's coming.*

She pressed the other call button again and again, as though she could hurry the second elevator by doing so.

Eight…nine…ten…

He's almost here!

Steph threw herself back at the security door and tried to key in the override code that would let her back in the lab after she'd punched in All Clear for the Night.

Her mind blanked. "What is it?" She fumbled at the little round numbers. "Oh-four-four-six-nine, right?'' The door didn't click. The light flickered red, warning her that another wrong code would freeze the lock for the night. "Come on, you bastard," she snarled. "I bought you. I programmed you. Let me in!" She miskeyed again.

The lock buzzed angrily and the red light shone solid. She wasn't getting in before morning.

Eleven...twelve...

Steph suddenly remembered the little gray canister in her purse—required equipment for any woman working in or near Chinatown. She scrambled for it. Grabbed it.

Thirteen...*ding!*

Screaming at the top of her lungs as her two-week self-defense class had taught her, Steph leaped for the widening crack in the elevator doors and aimed the nozzle directly at her attacker's face with one hand while she swung her purse with the other.

And at the last moment saw the surprise in his familiar golden-brown eyes.

WHILE HIS MIND was still grappling with the sight of Stephanie Alberts attacking him with pepper spray in one hand and a leather purse in the other, Reid automatically chopped the canister out of her hand and tossed it toward a corner of the elevator, noting as he did so that it hadn't fired because she'd failed to flip the safety. Once she was unarm—

Bonk! The elevator tilted when something impossibly heavy thumped him upside the head, and Stephanie's face—now looking more horrified than afraid, with her mouth making a big round O of surprise, loomed in front of him.

"Detective Peters!"

Afraid she might belt him with her purse again, Reid grabbed her wrist and stepped back, directly on top of the pepper spray. The metal canister shot out from underneath him and he flailed backward with one hand while the other pulled Stephanie with him on the way down.

They landed in a tangle of arms and legs, half in and half out of the elevator door, which dinged impatiently when it tried to shut itself on his kidneys. Stephanie struggled to right herself, nearly unmanning him with a pointy kneecap. Reid grabbed her upper arms and tangled his legs with hers in self-defense before barking, "Quit it!" when she kept squirming. "You're okay!"

What the hell was going on?

He shook her again, hoping to get through and she stilled. Froze. Seemed to realize where they were and how. Reid could feel her soft round breasts pressed against his chest, and he could swear he could feel her heart start to pound as the possibilities dawned on her.

Or maybe that was his heart, tempered only by the cop in him that remembered she'd been geared for attack when the elevator doors had opened. Though he could neither see nor sense immediate danger, he could feel it thrum through her body and into his.

Or maybe that was something else. Something far more dangerous. Far more insidious.

"It's okay," he repeated as the warmth spread and he felt her body soften as his did the opposite. He lowered his voice, "I'm here, Stephanie. You're safe."

It was the wrong thing to say, he could feel the change in her, though he couldn't have explained it. She tensed, and he hoped she hadn't just realized that he kept his gun in a shoulder holster, not his pocket. When she pushed herself off him and stood, the imprint of her soft curves hummed along his nerve endings like fire.

"I'm sorry, Detective Peters. I..." He could see the shields slam back down, could see her tuck her problems back into that place he couldn't reach and resisted the urge to bare his teeth. "I'm sorry. Being up here alone gives me the creeps sometimes, especially after what happened last year."

And by God, she wasn't a half-bad liar. She brushed at her sleeves and patted her riotous red hair as though proper grooming would prove that everything was just fine.

Nothing to see here. Move along.

Reid stood and resisted the urge to grab her shoulders. He wasn't sure whether he wanted to kiss her or shake her. Or both.

When he glanced pointedly at the pepper spray, she shrugged. "I don't usually work this late, and it was so deserted, and the phone kept ringing—" She broke off. "Anyway, I'm very sorry I tried to spray you. Lucky for both of us it didn't work. Although..."

She frowned. "If you'd been anyone else I'd have been in trouble."

He bent and picked up the offending canister. "You forgot to flip the safety off." He demonstrated. "See?" Then he tossed it back to her, not caring to ask whether she had a permit. He'd rather she have it than not, given the neighborhood they both worked in.

Now that there was no longer a body obstructing their path, the elevator doors whooshed shut. Irritated with both of them—and particularly with the fact that he could practically taste her on his lips though they'd never kissed, Reid jabbed the button marked Lobby before he turned on her. "What's going on, Stephanie? What's wrong? You can tell me. I'm your friend."

He meant it. He wanted to help. He hadn't even told Sturgeon about the Makepeace DNA. He'd said only that it was delayed.

Surprisingly, she snorted. "Yeah, and I have great taste when it comes to choosing guys to place my trust in." She leaned back in the elevator car and crossed her arms. "Why are you here, Detective Peters? Checking on your test results again? I told you I'd have them in a few days."

Reid thought of her embezzling ex-husband Luis. He thought of the ex-boyfriend who'd used her to gain access to the Watson lab and almost killed her when she was no longer useful. How could he possibly say, *but I'm different?*

And was he really so different? He carried a gun.

He knew how to disappear in Chinatown and how to find information down by Boston Harbor. He dreamed of blood and of a little girl's hollow, dead eyes, and when he woke all he wanted to do was curse and hit something like his old man used to do.

She was right. She shouldn't trust him. He wasn't any different than the others. But he still had a job to do.

The doors slid open. It was the end of the line.

She was out in a flash, but he caught her by the arm and tried not to think he'd touched more soft female flesh in the previous two minutes than in the prior year.

He steered her toward the big revolving doors at the front of the building, though she'd been headed for the back exit. "I thought I'd walk you home." He could make sure she made it safely. Make sure Maureen and the kid were okay.

Make that damn itch go away.

She balked. "You needn't bother, Detective Peters. I've been getting to and from work for several years now. I know the way."

"How about I come over for coffee then?"

"No." She tried edging around him toward the back exit again, but he held firm and sighed. She wasn't going to make it easy for him.

"We could have coffee down at the station, but I'm sure yours is much better. What do you say?"

As he had long suspected, Stephanie Alberts was anything but stupid. "A threat, Detective? On what basis?"

He touched a hand to the tender spot on his cheekbone. What the hell did she carry in that purse, anyway? "Assaulting a detective, for one." Seeing she was not inclined toward sympathy, he finally said, "And tampering with evidence, Stephanie." Her face drained of color and she swayed. For a quick moment he thought she might faint.

But she didn't. She narrowed her eyes. "And just what do you mean by that?"

So she was going to tough it out. "I saw the Makepeace film on your desk. The markers didn't line up. The DNA isn't a match. You're deliberately obstructing my investigation and I want to know why."

"Oh, and you're an expert at reading DNA fingerprints now, are you?"

Truth or bluff? Reid wasn't sure he could tell any more. He shook his head. "Of course not, but Dr. Watson explained them to me once and they seemed pretty easy. Either the bars line up or they don't."

Her lovely jade eyes narrowed even further. "Ever hear of an artifact, *Doctor* Peters?"

He shook his head. "Not in the context we're talking about, no."

"Well, genius, it just so happens that if the thermocycler temperature is wrong when the experiment is run, you can get nonspecific interactions called artifacts. They'll show up when you develop the film, but not before. They're not real results. Just garbage."

"Oh, come on," he fired back. "That sounds…"

Plausible. Hell.

He frowned. "Then you mean…?"

She nodded, and a little bit of smugness crept into her expression, pushing the other emotions aside. "That film you oh-so-cleverly snitched off my desk didn't mean a thing. Like I told you before, you'll have to wait until the end of the week for the test results."

Truth or lie?

"Now… You want to tell me why you thought it necessary to scrounge around my desk? How would you like it if I went through that notebook of yours?"

He'd be damned if he'd apologize for doing his job. But he felt the anger recede a bit and wondered whether she might not be telling the truth after all.

He shrugged. "I'd probably have—" *kittens.* Which reminded him. "Oh, hell. She Devil."

The little calico cat had been asleep in his underwear drawer late last night when he'd stopped by the house to change his clothes before heading to the station. She looked like she'd swallowed a football and it had gotten stuck. Sideways.

That had been—he glanced at his watch—more than twenty hours earlier.

"I *beg* your pardon?" Stephanie Alberts drew herself up to her full, imposing height of about five-foot-nothing and tried to look down her nose at him. "*What* did you call me?"

If someone had asked him a month ago which came first, the job or a mangy stray cat, Reid would've laughed that it was even a question. Now he wavered. Stephanie kept insisting there was nothing wrong, and yet... He shook his head. "Not you. There's someone waiting for me at home and I'm late. Since you're okay, I think I'll go..." He gestured toward the revolving door and her eyes narrowed.

"I thought you wanted coffee."

Boiling water. Towels. Sharp, sterilized knife. His mind came up with a reasonable-sounding list of items. But what if something went wrong?

Growing up, he hadn't been allowed a pet. Hadn't even known he liked animals until the little scrap of orange and black and white fur had appeared on his fire escape in a blinding rainstorm and howled until he let it in. She—and the size of the cat's stomach left no doubt that it was a she—had eaten an entire can of albacore tuna, scratched his hand and barfed on the ugly Oriental rug he'd inherited from the old man.

Reid was hooked.

He'd taken her to the vet, bought a bagful of expensive toys before figuring out that she preferred crumpled balls of wax paper, and after going through a whole box of Band-Aids in the first week, christened the beast She Devil.

He was expecting her to give birth to a litter of demons any minute now, but the blessed event had been pushed from his mind by his worry over a woman who quite clearly neither needed nor wanted his help.

"Detective Peters? Coffee?"

He shook his head. "Not right now, thanks."

Stephanie was fine. She'd explained the Makepeace film pretty convincingly, and as for the incident in the elevator, well, just about any woman steeling herself to walk through Chinatown at night could be excused for being nervous—especially considering what had happened in that very lab just the previous year. "Okay then, can I give you a lift home?"

She shook her head vehemently. "No thanks. You just be on your way, and—"

STEPHANIE WAS TALKING to thin air. Peters had practically sprinted out the revolving door to the street. She blew out a breath and unknotted her fingers from the purse.

This is what she'd wanted, right? She'd wanted him to go away and leave her alone. She'd hoped he would buy the "artifact" story she'd cooked up after she'd glanced over from her phone conversation and seen him looking at the Makepeace film. She'd prayed he wouldn't insist on driving—or worse, walking her home, leaving her to make the voice on the phone believe that she hadn't told him anything.

"So this is a good thing," she told herself firmly. "He's gone and I can go home."

Then why did she feel like scratching the eyes out of the woman Detective Peters was running to? Why did she feel such a twisting sense of betrayal that he'd asked her for coffee when he had someone waiting for him?

"Not everyone says *coffee* and means *sex*, Stephanie," she lectured herself sternly. Her face flushed at the word and her skin heated at the memory of the good, solid bulk of the detective's body beneath hers in the elevator and the heavy warmth that had stolen through her. The quick throb of her pulse as their limbs intertwined, and…and she'd sworn off men for good.

You have terrible taste, she told herself, *don't even go there. And besides, you've done nothing but lie to Detective Peters for the last twelve hours. That's not exactly a great basis for a lasting relationship.*

Or a brief, explosive one. The thought brought a quick liquid heat.

"You okay, Miss Alberts?" She jolted and shot a glance at the back hall of the lobby, relaxing when she saw the night watchman's familiar stocky form. Though thoughts of the handsome detective were a momentary distraction, the fear that the man on the phone was watching her stayed near. Lurked.

"I'm fine, Bobby." When had the words *I'm fine* become a mantra? "Just heading home." She looked out past the revolving glass doors and suppressed a shudder. She didn't want to go home through the Zone. Not tonight.

"It's late, Miss Alberts, why don't you take the catwalk over to the train station? It'll be safer."

She seized the idea gratefully. Usually, she spurned the T because the hospital was a mere ten-minute walk from her house and it took twice that to wait for the train. But tonight the brightly lit, well-guarded MBTA station seemed like heaven. "I'll do that, Bobby. Thank you."

So she took the catwalk and waited for the train. But the feeling of being watched didn't go away.

LATER THAT NIGHT, Reid trotted up the old granite steps and banged on the nail-studded door with the cast-iron knocker. There was something to be said for the charm of the Patriot District, he thought as he scanned the narrow cobbled street. There were flower boxes at every window overflowing with period-correct plantings, and a discreet kiosk on the corner filled with brochures.

A sweet slide of saxophone drifted out of the window next door, making Reid think of beignets and open-air cafés.

Though the neighborhoods were only fifteen minutes apart by foot, Patriot was a far cry from the open markets and seedy underbelly of Chinatown. He wasn't sure which he preferred.

He knocked again, and a little wooden window opened in the big wooden door. Jade-green eyes stared out at him.

"Well, that's not very safe," he commented. "I could stick a gun right through there and start shooting. Aren't peepholes considered historically accurate around here? They're certainly safer. You never know who's going to come knocking."

The eyes blinked. Then Steph's voice said, "You're absolutely right. I'll keep it closed from now on."

The little window slid shut.

It took him a full minute to realize she wasn't going to open the door.

He knocked again, harder, and started to feel prickles on the back of his neck. On the pretext of scratching his head, he scanned the neat neighborhood again. Nothing. Patriot might be pretty to look at, but there were certainly plenty of places to hide.

Or else he needed a vacation. A long one, with sun and beaches, and curvy redheads wearing string bikinis.

Or lab coats.

"Stephanie? I need to talk to you." He knocked, and kept knocking until he heard a dead bolt being shot from inside.

"Go away," she said, then contradicted herself by opening the door. "What do you want?"

"Coffee," he said, and pushed his way into the house. "Your aunt here?"

"No. But why don't you come in and make yourself at home?" she offered sarcastically as he prowled through the first floor and found nothing amiss. "Maureen's out for the evening."

He found Stephanie's daughter in the living room, playing quietly with a model horse and a stuffed bear. She was galloping the bear around with the horse on the bear's back. He supposed it made sense to a three-year-old.

"Hey, kid," he said, because it seemed rude not to acknowledge her, and the girl gave him a blinding smile that lit her whole face and shifted something inside his chest.

God! That human beings could ever do something evil to a child. He felt suddenly small, tainted by the things he'd seen. The things he'd done.

When the little girl stood up and walked toward him, Reid took a step back and bumped into Stephanie. The brief contact reminded him of their almost-clinch in the elevator, and the shadows in her eyes reminded him of questions still unanswered.

She quirked a smile. "Don't like kids much?"

"It's not that. It's just—" He shrugged. "I guess I don't see them at their best too often, you know?"

"Too many tantrums?"

Too much blood, he thought. Too many babies hanging on their mothers' legs while their daddies were dragged out the front door. But he said, "Something like that." Noticing that Stephanie was holding a pair of mugs, he reached for one. "Thanks."

At her invitation, he sat on a stiff-looking old-fashioned chair that startled him by being comfortable. Stephanie sat on the sofa. She sipped her drink. "Why are you here, Detective? Wasn't your... company glad to see you?"

Reid glanced at the four parallel scratches on his arm. "She wasn't in a very good mood. I think she's feeling fat."

There was a little tug at his pant leg, and an inquiring noise, like a small bird chirping. He looked down at the kid. Her lips were pursed, and another chirp emerged. "She whistles?"

Stephanie nodded. "Maureen said she started it

this morning. We're hoping it's a sign that she's getting ready to talk again.''

The girl frowned as though concentrating, and warbled a few more notes.

''Almost a song,'' he said for lack of anything more profound to say. He wished she would go lean on her mother's leg. He was finding the warm, heavy press of her little body more than a bit distracting. To ward off the sudden urge to reach down and lift the kid into his lap, he took a healthy slug of coffee, hoping he'd burn his tongue and shock himself back to rationality.

The liquid—which absolutely, positively wasn't coffee—seared its way down his throat and set up a nice, cozy fire in his stomach. He coughed hard, and was relieved when the noise sent the kid scuttling over to her mother. ''God! What is this?'' He glared at the inoffensive mug, which had a cartoon dog playing the guitar, with the slogan Rock and Roll! on it.

Stephanie put a hand to her mouth. He was pretty sure she was trying to hide a grin, though the little wrinkle between her eyebrows remained. ''Um. Hot chocolate?''

''Have a little hot chocolate with your liqueur, why don't you?''

She lifted her daughter up to her lap. Dark hair shone against red curls. Liquid-brown eyes glittered beside jade-green. For a moment, Reid wished he still painted. Then he wished he could get a grip on himself. He was losing it.

"Maureen makes chocolate for me when I'm stressed." Stephanie shrugged. "I guess I just reached for it automatically. I can make coffee if you'd prefer."

"Stressed?" It gave him the opening he'd been looking for. He should've been at home, waiting for kittens and watching the Sox whup the tar out of the Indians, but instead he'd gone out for a bag of cheese puffies and wound up on her doorstep.

Call it a hunch.

Call it an excuse, whispered a little voice in the back of his head.

He didn't have an answer for the voice in his head, and Stephanie didn't seem to have an answer for him.

"Stephanie?" He waited until she looked up. Their eyes held as he said, "You can trust me. Tell me what's wrong."

She frowned. "Nothing is wrong. How many times do I have to tell you that? I'm fine."

She shot to her feet and slung Jilly on her hip, and Reid set his mug aside and stood as well, trying to figure out if Stephanie was afraid or annoyed. The little girl watched him with solemn eyes. Her lips pursed and she whistled that same string of notes. Damned if it didn't sound like a song, but it wasn't any song he knew.

"I think you'd better go now, Detective Peters." Steph's voice made an attempt at being level. "I need to put Jilly to bed. Pull the door shut on your way out, please."

She marched up the stairs toward her daughter's

room and Reid took a step to follow. Then he stopped himself.

What was he doing?

She'd told him nothing was wrong. She'd explained the test results from that morning. There was no reason to believe that Jilly's disappearing act had been anything other than a field trip.

And she'd asked him to leave.

"Give it up, Peters," he told himself sternly. "There's nothing fishy going on here and the woman's made it plain as day that she's not interested in you. Go home."

Could it be that the itch between his shoulder blades had been displaced from somewhere a little farther south, and that he'd been making up excuses to see her?

Yeah, he admitted, more than likely. Since that first day he'd seen her at the Watson lab, wrapped in that ridiculous white coat and worried for her boss, Stephanie Alberts had lurked around the edges of his mind. When she'd been hurt during the course of his investigation, he'd blamed guilt for the compulsion that had him sitting at her bedside when he was off duty.

"Don't be an idiot," he told himself. "Go home." He heard the water in the upstairs bathroom shut off. He tried not to picture the young mother helping her daughter brush her teeth. Tucking the dark-haired child into bed.

Kissing her goodnight.

He thought of the little girl he hadn't saved, and

knew that if Stephanie and Jilly were okay, the best place for him was far away from them both.

For their sake and his.

He spun on his heel, headed for the door—

And heard Stephanie scream.

Chapter Four

Reid spun and bolted up the stairs, yanking his weapon clear of the shoulder holster as the screams rang through the narrow house like a Halloween soundtrack. He collided with Stephanie in the hall as she ran out of her daughter's bedroom, clutching Jilly, who'd begun to wail.

Steph flung herself at him and pressed her face into his chest. She was drawing in big, sobbing gulps of air and he pulled her close with his free arm, holding the gun well away from mother and child. The rage sang through him, and the need to protect.

Hearing no movement from the bedroom, Reid pressed them against the far wall of the hallway. ''Stay here.''

He peeked into the room, and seeing that it was empty, stepped all the way in and fanned the small space with his weapon. The window was open, the ruffled white curtains blowing inward on the slight night breeze. He stepped across and looked down. Nothing out there except a hundred dark, historical hiding places.

"All clear," he said to nobody in particular, before hearing a commotion on the stairs. A man's raised voice.

Stephanie!

Forgetting caution, forgetting training and unleashing the rage, Reid leapt out of the bedroom into the hall. "Stop, police!"

And ducked as a saxophone whistled through the air where his head had just been. Reid plastered himself against the wall, repeating, "Police!"

His attacker froze and Reid found himself pointing his gun at a large, grizzled black man with a hoop in one ear, a faded marine tattoo on the opposite bicep, and a saxophone cocked on his shoulder like a baseball bat.

Stephanie leapt between them. "Detective Peters! Mortimer! No!"

Even before Stephanie's quick cry, Reid was lowering his weapon, having seen Maureen on the big guy's heels. With no immediate threat apparent, he tucked his gun back out of sight and returned to the bedroom while a babble of voices erupted in the hallway.

"What's wrong? Steph, what happened? We—I heard you scream. Are you okay?" Maureen's questions tumbled over each other, but Reid barely registered them as he scanned the little ruffled room.

Stuffed animals. A jumble of toys on the floor. Frilly white bed.

A teddy bear's bodyless head placed on the center of the bed, and the words Do It spelled out in grotesque letters formed from the elegant, spindly legs that had been broken off a herd of model horses.

Reid checked the window. The historically correct latch had been popped.

Child's play.

He walked back into the hall, where Maureen was alternately soothing Jilly and asking her niece questions while Stephanie stared blankly into the bedroom, looking shocked.

Well hell, that was fine with him. Now maybe she'd tell him what was going on, because this was sure as hell no artifact. He pulled his cell from his pocket and called the incident in to Patriot while battling the ridiculous urge to stroke Stephanie's hair and tell her everything was going to be okay.

Empty words. He didn't have a clue what was going on.

Stupid words. He wasn't sure he could fix it even if he knew. But he was sure as hell going to try. It was his job.

''They'll be here in a few minutes,'' he said to the others. ''Maureen, is there somewhere you can take Jilly for the night? Somewhere nearby?'' Though she was a flutterer by nature, Reid had learned that Maureen could be a rock when she needed to be. She merely nodded.

The big, black ex-marine with the saxophone and the earring stepped forward and introduced himself as their next-door neighbor, Mortimer. ''I'll take the little peanut and *her*—'' he cut a glance at Maureen and Reid felt the tension hum ''—home with me for a while. We'll be there when you need us.''

Maureen huffed a bit, but agreed ''if only so Jilly could have some peace and quiet.'' Once they'd gone, Reid steered Stephanie downstairs and stuffed her in a kitchen chair, ready to drag the answers out of her if necessary.

He glanced at the hot chocolate and made coffee instead.

When he returned to the table, she had tears running down her face. Her shoulders were shaking with silent sobs.

He placed a mug in front of her and sat. ''Artifacts, right? Everything's fine, right? Nothing to worry about, why don't you head on home, Detective Peters, right? What the hell's going on, Stephanie?''

Though he wanted nothing more than to pull her into his arms and let her cry it out on his chest, he knew it wasn't the right time. Knew she wasn't the right woman.

The Patriot cops arrived then, and Reid took a moment to explain the situation—what little he knew of it. When they'd headed upstairs to begin the routine of evidence collection, he returned to the kitchen, only to find that she had rebuilt her defenses while he was out of the room.

''You needn't be too bothered, Detective Peters. It was probably just a prank.'' She sipped the coffee and grimaced. Her fingers were pale shadows on the white mug that she held with two hands to keep it from shaking.

"Bull," he said bluntly, and had the satisfaction of seeing her flinch. "Pranks in Patriot are limited to replacing the Stars and Stripes with British flags on the anniversary of the Boston Tea Party." Although Reid remembered the Patriot cops talking about the neighborhood's uproar, he'd thought it a fine joke at the time. "Kids around here don't break second-story windows to write messages with broken toys." And leave a headless teddy bear that had given even Reid the creeps. It was too close to the little girl. He took a breath and tried to keep his voice level when he wanted to shout. "I'm not buying it. Try again."

She shook her head. "I don't have to try again, Detective Peters. Like I said, it was a prank. Nothing more."

Burning impatience bloomed from Reid's left shoulder blade and skittered through his body. His fingers tingled as he gripped her upper arms and dragged her up. The kitchen chair clattered as it fell to the tiled floor behind her.

He felt like shaking her until she told him the truth. He felt like kissing her until the truth didn't matter any more.

Instead, he picked her up clean off the floor and held her at his eye level. He glared and said, "Swear to me you don't know why this happened. Swear to me you're not in any danger, and I'll walk out your front door and never bother you again. Swear it."

Stephanie stared into his eyes, and he into hers, and when her answer came, it wasn't the one he'd expected.

She kissed him.

IT WAS AN IMPULSE born of desperation, of deception, but once she'd acted on the mad urge a wholly different array of feelings rose up and swamped Steph with a wash of sensation.

His lips were softer than she might have imagined for a man who'd charged up the stairs with a neat, deadly looking gun in his hand, ready to protect Jilly and her from a headless teddy bear and a pile of maimed model horses.

Make me tell you about the man on the phone, her mind whispered as she deepened the kiss, sliding her tongue along the seam of his lips until they parted and he let her in. He tasted of strong coffee and a hint of chocolate, and as he leaned back and dropped her suspended weight so gravity pressed them together chest to chest, hip to hip, she wanted to say, *Make me tell you. Make me trust you.* She needed to tell someone. Needed to trust someone. She didn't want to lie any more. Didn't want to be alone any more.

With her hands trapped between their bodies, she strained closer to him as a kiss meant only to distract him became something more.

Memories of Luis's slick, practiced self-absorption and Roger's mechanical detachment were torn away in a surge of raw, powerful greed. *More.* She wanted more, in the way the girl she'd once been had wanted more, before disappointment and disillusionment had taught her to accept so much less.

Stephanie curled her trapped hands into his button-down shirt and pulled, baring a V of rough male flesh. She purred into his mouth and thought she felt his hands tremble where they gripped her upper arms.

She'd known it would be like this between them. She'd known since the first moment she'd seen him, asking his professionally detached questions while the horror of what had happened to Genie Watson in the darkroom lurked at the back of his eyes, and his need to find the perpetrator burned in him like flame.

Though she'd just started dating Roger, Stephanie had taken one look at the intense detective with the strange amber eyes, and had yearned for something she couldn't have. Couldn't name.

Then Roger had betrayed her. Or perhaps she'd betrayed herself by falling so completely for a murderer, for a man who beat her into a coma when she had discovered him outside Genie's house and recognized his face.

When she'd awakened in the hospital and seen Reid Peters at her bedside, she'd thought, *Thank God, he's here.* Then she'd realized that he was there to take her statement, and that her poor judgment had nearly gotten her and Genie killed.

She'd given her statement in monosyllables and turned her head away. She'd been so ashamed.

But she wouldn't turn away now. She pressed closer to him, feeling the blood, muscle and bone beneath her fingertips as though it was her own.

Her child was safe with Mortimer. Her aunt as well. She couldn't stop the voice on the phone from knowing that the police had come to her house. She couldn't change it now. She could only take pleasure in this kiss, knowing that the dawn would come soon enough, and with it all the problems she'd had the day before, and more.

He loosened his grip on her upper arms and started to let her slide to the floor. Still locked lip to lip, Stephanie felt them both shudder as her breasts rubbed along his chest, as her thighs slid along his legs, and—

Boots thudded on the stairs.

She jumped away from him just as a small herd of uniformed officers tramped into the kitchen.

"We're all done up there, Detective, and…" The elder uniform trailed off as he took in the state of Peters's shirt and the almost palpable energy buzzing in the room. Steph felt a wash of heat bloom on her cheeks, which felt raspy and raw from his stubble. "Problem in here?" the uniform asked with a sparkle in his faded gray eyes.

"No! No problem at all, officers. Detective Peters was just…" Steph trailed off, not thinking clearly enough to come up with a believable lie, and feeling heartily sick of the need. She'd done nothing but lie for the last twenty-four hours.

"Doing nothing that is any of Patriot's business," Peters filled in smoothly. He aimed a glare at the uniforms. "Got it?" When they nodded with knowing grins, he glanced over at Steph. "And you can call me Reid."

THE UNIFORMS left not long after, and once the black and white was gone, Maureen called to see if she and Jilly could come home. She swore the child couldn't sleep because their neighbor's mynah bird kept singing dirty limericks, but from the look on Mortimer's face when he walked the ladies home, Reid supposed there was a bit more to it than that.

"Are you sure you don't want to stay at my place, at least until the upstairs window's fixed?" the mountainous ex-marine asked once they were inside the house.

Stephanie was engrossed in cuddling her daughter, so Maureen answered for both of them. "No, thank you, Mortimer. We'll be fine with Reid here."

"You will?" Reid was just as surprised as Mortimer. He hadn't been thinking of staying. He'd been planning on stopping by his apartment for a quick check on She Devil before heading to the station to see whether there had been any similar stuffed animal beheadings in the city.

Though he hadn't objected to her method of distraction, it hadn't escaped Reid's attention that Stephanie had avoided his questions. But *lord*, what a distraction. The anger that had twisted in his gut had exploded in an instant into a white-hot lust like none he'd ever felt before. From the moment her lips had touched his, he'd felt like some sort of primitive, powerful caveman dangling his prize in the air while he had his way. Only he hadn't been alone in the project—she'd been fully involved in the pillaging...

"Right, Detective Peters?"

"What?" He snapped back to the reality of four pairs of eyes watching him questioningly and a pair of pants that were beginning to take on a life of their own. He coughed and shoved his hands in his pockets. "Yes, of course."

Maureen nodded in satisfaction. "You see, Mortimer? Detective Peters will stay the night, so you don't have to worry your crew cut over us."

"Detective Peters needn't stay," Stephanie objected. "We'll be fine."

Which is why she was clutching the kid like she might disappear at any moment. Keeping his hands firmly in his pockets lest he be tempted to shake the truth out of her—or drag her upstairs, whichever she preferred—Reid shook his head. "Your aunt is right—that upstairs window isn't secure. I think your daughter should sleep with you tonight. I'll stay in her room in case the perp comes back to mess up any more toys—" or some people "—and I'll call a locksmith I know in the morning. He'll fix the window." And install historically inaccurate dead bolts on every point of access, whether Stephanie liked it or not.

At the mention of her toys, the little girl's lower lip trembled. Her dark hair was sticking out in all directions and she looked pretty miserable. Reid had to fight the sudden desire to give the kid a hug and tell her it was going to be okay. It was just as well he resisted, because a moment later she started to cry, and for such a quiet kid Jilly Alberts cried *loud*.

Unable to argue with him over the escalating

wails, Stephanie finally glared at Reid, huffed, "Fine!" and carried her daughter upstairs to bed with Maureen at her heels. The cries abated some with distance and walls, and Reid let out a grateful breath.

"So you'll stay?"

Reid cocked an eyebrow at Mortimer, feeling like he'd been set up, but not nearly as annoyed as he might have been by the prospect. "Seems so." He paused, looked the big, capable-looking man up and down. "You see anything unusual this afternoon? This evening?"

"Nah." The hoop in Mortimer's ear glinted as he shook his head. "Would've told the other cops if I had. But," he paused and looked sideways at Reid, "I had a sort of...*feeling* about eight o'clock. Know what I mean?"

"Yeah," Reid said, resisting the urge to scratch his back. "I do."

"You think this had anything to do with Jilly *wandering* off yesterday?" The way Mortimer said it made Reid think the ex-marine didn't like the story any more than he did. "Because Maureen didn't have her eyes off the little tyke for more than a second, and she and I both scoured the park right after she vanished. She wasn't there."

"It's still under investigation." Reid fell back on the standard line.

"And?" Mortimer wasn't buying the evasion any more than Reid had forgotten about the questions Stephanie hadn't answered earlier.

Reid shrugged. "And I've got a feeling of my own." He glanced upstairs as blessed quiet reigned once again.

Mortimer nodded. "I'll take the daytime watch then. I don't have to play at the pub until tomorrow evening, so I can hang around here. It'll drive Maureen crazy," he didn't seem bothered by the prospect. "Stephanie should be safe enough at the lab."

Reid didn't bother pointing out that Boston General hadn't proven itself the safest of hideouts in the past. He simply nodded, knowing where he'd be the next day. "Good to meet you then, Mortimer."

The large black man nodded his gray-frosted head. "Nice meeting you, too, Peters, though I might've wished it was under other circumstances." He headed for the door, tossing over his shoulder, "Oh, and you might want to know that your shirt's missing a button, Detective."

Reid ground his teeth as the door closed on Mortimer's reminder of his lapse. Anger rose, but it wasn't the familiar impotent rage he battled on a daily basis. He was mad at himself. Not only had he kissed a witness and a victim, he'd kissed a woman who had lied to him about an ongoing investigation.

He scrubbed his hands through his hair and blew out a frustrated breath as the taste of her swam through his body like a drug. It wouldn't happen again, he told himself as his heart pounded out the message on the little girl's bed.

It *couldn't* happen again. If his father had taught

him nothing else, it was that there was nothing more important than the job. Not family. Not happiness.

And especially not love.

UPSTAIRS, STEPHANIE lay in her bed and stared at the ceiling while her mind conjured up dead, dark eyes in the corners of the room and she shivered with dread. What would the voice do now? He had to know the police were in the house.

She reached out and touched the curls on her sleeping daughter's head. Safe. For now.

Steph shuddered. She'd almost hoped the harsh, oily voice would call so she could tell him that she hadn't turned over the true DNA results to the police. So she could explain why Reid was there.

And perhaps explain it to herself as well.

Steph rolled over and punched her pillow for good measure. She was hot and itchy, and the still weight of the child sleeping beside her in the bed didn't bring her the usual comfort.

She lay still for a moment, listening to the dark. Thinking of Reid. Thinking of kissing him. Of how it had been everything she hadn't allowed herself to want and more, because she had found an unexpected sweetness in him beneath the layer of tough cop and man. Of how she couldn't afford to think that way when she was bound and determined to deceive him, even though the kiss had reawakened parts of her that had lain dormant ever since that first night Luis had come home smelling of cheap wine and perfume and cursed at her when she complained.

It had not been a tender kiss, but she hadn't needed tender. Hadn't wanted it. She had wanted the rush of pure heat to burn through her and leave nothing behind—not lies, not fear, not anything.

And she'd gotten more than she bargained for. If it hadn't been for the interruption…

She blew out a frustrated breath, rolled over in the bed and punched the pillow again, feeling hot and churned up.

After their kiss, Peters had huddled with the Patriot cops and Steph had put Jilly down to sleep and brushed her teeth. She had glanced at the ratty white lab coat that usually served as her robe, and changed into a flowing blue satin nightgown that covered more than a ball gown, but clung in all the right places. Luis had hated the nightgown, and that alone was enough to make it one of her favorite articles of clothing, though it hadn't seen any action since he'd gone.

Then again, neither had she. Her one attempt at a relationship since had been Roger. She had—thankfully—never slept with him.

So she'd smoothed the soft blue material over her hips and belly, feeling daring. Feeling safe and terrified at the same time. Feeling confused and thinking she was a terrible person to think of her daughter's safety and the detective's tight backside in the same breath. Then she lay down beside her daughter and waited for sleep to come. Waited for him to come.

And waited.

And waited.

The house was silent. The grandmother clock in the downstairs hall bonged occasionally in a random pattern that had absolutely nothing to do with the actual time. Normally she found it charming. Tonight it annoyed her, especially when she was sure it had been at least an hour since she'd heard any movement in the house and longer since the phone had last rung.

The voice wasn't going to call. The detective wasn't going to beckon her into the hallway.

And there was no way in hell she was getting any sleep.

"Darn it." She sighed again and thought of hot chocolate, a poor substitute for safety or sex, but as close as she was likely to come to either for the night. On the way to the kitchen, she glanced into Jilly's room, almost afraid of seeing a shadowy figure waiting in there with a dark, oily voice and a thirst for little girls.

She froze at the moon-gilded shadow.

Peters lay sprawled across Jilly's bed in a jumble of ruffles and stuffed animals. Fast asleep.

Steph stepped farther into the room. She couldn't help herself. The light from the hall played across the hard planes of his face, softening them and making him look younger. More vulnerable. When he was awake, it was hard to get past the golden, almost wolfish color of his eyes.

As he slept, she thought she could see the hint of a dimple on one cheek. She wondered why she'd never noticed it before, and had to stop herself from reaching out to touch.

His shirt was open where she had pulled at it during that wild, wanton kiss, and Steph thought that if she lay down on Jilly's tiny bed beside him, she could rest her head against his shoulder and touch her tongue to that V of exposed flesh.

Then she saw his badge lying open on the child-sized night table. She stepped back toward the doorway.

Her track record was horrible. Her taste ran to liars and thieves. And to make it worse, this time *she* was the liar and the lawbreaker. She had no choice.

She had made her decision. She was going to send an innocent man to prison for a rape he hadn't committed. The alternative was unthinkable and Jilly and Maureen had to be protected at all costs. But law-abiding, justice-defending Reid Peters would never understand. He didn't like kids and he didn't believe in letting the bad guys win.

He'd never forgive her for what she was planning to do the next day. Never. And knowing that was harder than she'd thought it would be, because it meant there could never be more between them than a single kiss in her kitchen.

She backed toward the doorway, turned and went back to her own room, curled around her daughter and willed herself to sleep. Willed herself not to cry.

REID WATCHED her go through slitted eyelids and wondered at the play of emotions on her face.

A brief stint undercover had left him with a wicked scar high on his right thigh and an aversion to being snuck up on while asleep, so he'd come instantly awake when she'd paused in the doorway. Having taken a necessary moment to identify the intruder and shift his hand away from the gun he'd stuck under a pillow shaped like a purple dragon, Reid had feigned sleep, curious about what she'd do next.

At first, her face had looked tender, almost madonna-like. Then he'd seen a flash of something that might have been desire. The nipples beneath that slinky blue satin had slid into view for a bare moment, and not all of his body parts had stayed as still as he might have liked. But then her expression had shifted yet again to wariness. Fear.

Deception.

She'd backed from the room and he'd let her go, knowing that in the morning he would take her to the station and make it official. She was the job now, not the woman. It had to be that way. *He* had to be that way.

Restless now, half–aroused by the sight of her in that long cool slide of blue satin and the rest of the way hard from the memory of their kiss in the kitchen, Reid prowled down the stairs and rechecked the pitiful locks on the ground-floor windows. The routine soothed him and he felt the cop's calm descend. It was a shield of sorts, built to keep him apart from the horrors he saw every day, built to protect others from the rage that rose within him.

Perhaps tonight the shield would save him from himself.

He prowled back upstairs and heard a soft noise, like a bird chirping. It drew him down the length of the hall.

The sound came again, seven notes, a pause, then a repeat. Reid relaxed a fraction. It was the kid whistling again.

Telling himself it was just to make sure they were both okay, Reid stepped inside the bedroom and was instantly surrounded by the scent of female flesh and baby powder.

Stephanie.

The job. She was the job now. She could be nothing more.

The soft glow of moonlight outlined mother and child. Stephanie was sound asleep atop the covers, the blue satin cupped around curves enough to make a man beg. The gown had fallen aside at the high slit, showing off a long, tapered leg.

Chirp?

A pair of eyes gleamed in the darkness as the little girl peered over the dip at her mother's waist. Reid waggled his fingers and held one to his lips, then pointed down at Steph. "Mommy's sleeping," he mouthed, and the child nodded solemnly. She held up her arms.

She wanted to be picked up? Reid shuddered. He'd rather walk into an armed camp of drug smugglers in his underwear.

Ignoring her gesture, he sat down on a rocking

chair beside the bed. It protested with a loud creak, and the little girl giggled, high and sweet. Steph shifted and murmured in her sleep, and Reid gave in to temptation and stroked her cheek, feeling his heart turn over in his chest when she smiled.

Chirp? There was a tug at his wrinkled pant leg, and he looked down to discover that Jilly had somehow ended up on the floor, looking up at him. She raised her arms.

Oh hell, he thought, and lifted her up into his lap. How bad could it be? The anger was far away now, hidden under layers of unidentified emotion and worry and that cool cop calm.

Her body snuggled warm and trusting against his chest, and he shifted far enough to pull his cell phone out of his pocket and place it on the bedside table. When the material twisted around his body and annoyed him, Reid pulled the ruined shirt over his head and resettled her. He'd keep the gun at the small of his back for now, safe from sticky little fingers.

Her tiny heart tapped against the bare skin of his chest, and her sweet, soapy scent rose to his nostrils as he dozed in the rocking chair and listened for the danger he knew was out there. Somewhere.

STEPHANIE WAS DREAMING of ringing phones and dark voices that wanted her to do things. Terrible things.

Or I'll send her back to you in pieces...in pieces...in pieces.

Da-da-da-*DUM!* The shout of the phone catapulted

her to wakefulness and she grabbed it and felt her heart gallop painfully.

"H'lo?"

There was a loud silence in the background, a hiss and crackle of radios and the murmur of voices. She repeated, "Hello?" while her stomach knotted in anticipation of the voice. The threats. She reached across the bed, needing to touch Jilly.

Her hand met cool, empty sheets and she jolted upright as a someone said, "Is...um, is Peters there?"

The voice wasn't oily. It wasn't evil.

But it *was* familiar.

"That for me?" The lazy drawl snapped her eyes to her grandmother's rocking chair and the terror receded some when she saw her daughter there.

Fast asleep on Peters's bare chest.

Oh my. Was it possible to go from terror to white-hot desire in half a heartbeat? Apparently so.

He gestured toward the phone that had rung Beethoven and she watched the slide of muscle across his chest. "Want to give it to me, or would you prefer to take a message?"

She handed it over, took the warm weight of her daughter from him and tried not to stare. The dawn-gilded dips and hollows of the most perfect chest she could ever have imagined were marred by a long thin scar and a small constellation of three round marks high on his shoulder. *Cigarette burns,* her mind supplied from the endless reels of true-crime TV, and she thought with dull horror that they looked old. Old enough to have been made when he was a boy.

She wanted to press her lips to the marks and make them disappear. Make the hurt disappear. Wanted to trace the flat, dark bud of the nipple that drew up tightly as she watched it. Wanted to lose herself in the eyes that had turned to molten gold in the dawn.

She handed him the phone. "I think it's Detective Sturgeon."

The gold turned hard in an instant, and he nodded shortly, taking the phone and striding from the room, listening and grunting the occasional reply. Steph pressed a kiss to her sleeping child's brow as she gazed at his naked back and the gun tucked into his waistband.

Then she saw his bare shoulders tense. Heard him curse, low and violent, and knew something was very, very wrong. Again, she swung between terror and desire as though she was on a crazy carnival ride that wouldn't slow down. Wouldn't let her off.

Something had happened.

"I'll be right there." He snapped the phone shut so hard it sounded like a shot.

His wrinkled shirt was draped haphazardly over the back of the rocking chair and he grabbed it and pulled it on as he strode for the door. "I've got to go. I'll call Mortimer and have him keep an eye on this place. Take a cab to Boston General and I'll meet you there later. We need to talk."

Steph all but chased him down the hall, carrying

Jilly because she was afraid to put the little girl down. "Wait! What is it? What happened?"

What if the voice had hurt someone from the lab? What if he'd known she and Jilly were being guarded and had taken his revenge on someone else?

It would be her fault for not switching the results the day before. Her fault for letting Reid in the house. All her fault.

He turned back halfway down the stairs, though he was clearly in a rush. "It's a Chinatown call," he said, as though that explained everything.

The slam of the front door echoed through the house.

A moment later, the phone on the hallway table rang and Steph picked it up automatically, her mind still jumbled with frantic possibilities. "Hello?"

Maybe Reid was calling from the car to explain.

But no. The silence had a dark, dead quality and the fear barreled through her and left her shaking. She let Jilly slide down to the floor, wanting her as far away from the voice as possible. She looked out the window and saw Peters get in an unremarkable sedan. He wasn't on his cell phone. "Hello?"

The slow, soulless inflection was as familiar as her own heartbeat, she'd thought of it so often in the last day. "Morning, bitch. I hope you enjoyed your night with the cop. Peters, isn't it?" Stephanie shivered at the voice, at the menace and the knowledge. "Very cozy."

"I didn't—" Steph managed before her throat locked tight. Jilly was staring up, her eyes dark with fear and understanding beyond her years. "I didn't tell him anything," she said. "I told him he'd have to wait a few days for the results. I have to rerun the experiments to fix the results the way you want them." She was almost begging now as she felt the dawn break over her as though she was burning up with the fear. "I need more time, you have to believe me. I haven't told him anything. I swear!"

A considering silence. Then, "No matter, bitch. He's a part of this now, thanks to you. I left him a message. A present. I'm sure he'll thank you for it."

"But please, I—"

"No!" the voice practically roared. "It's too late to switch the results, bitch. The cops know too much. Now you need to lose the DNA. Lose it all and the records, too. Do it today, or you're dead. You, the kid, the old woman…maybe even the cop, too. Got it?" When she didn't answer right away, the voice screamed, *"Do you understand?"*

"I understand," Steph whispered after a moment. She looked down at her daughter and heard the buzzing in her ears that indicated that the line was dead.

Jilly looked up warily, as if to say, *What now?* and Steph bit back a hysterical sob.

What now?

Chapter Five

Sturgeon was waiting for Reid at the hotel, holding a fresh shirt and a candy cigar.

Reid buttoned the shirt and scowled at the cigar. Since Sturgeon's wife had insisted he trade cigarettes for mints, he had given out peppermint cigars for special occasions.

"I didn't get laid," Reid snarled at his partner. "And even if I had, it hasn't been so long that it rates a cigar."

Well, in truth, it had been a while—since last year, in fact, when Yvette had thrown him out and run his Italian leather jacket through the washing machine before she mailed it to him wrapped around a week-old salmon steak, but that still didn't mean he appreciated his partner marking the end of his celibacy.

Particularly when it hadn't ended.

"It's not for that, though I'll keep it in mind."

Reid glanced over as they were waved through the police line outside the China Gold motel, a seedy rent-by-the-hour dive three blocks from Boston General. "Then what's it for?"

Figuring it was almost the same as brushing his teeth, he bit off the end of the peppermint cigar.

Sturgeon clapped him on the back. "Congratulations! You're a daddy!" Of course, he yelled it loud enough for every uniform in the building to hear.

Reid scowled, then grinned as he figured it out. "The kittens! How many? Is she okay? Are they?"

As they followed the damp, swampy-smelling hallway into the bowels of the China Gold, Sturgeon grinned faintly. "Well, well, well. First you spend the night somewhere other than your place or your desk. Then a woman answers the phone—and don't think I didn't recognize the voice." He paused. Reid bit off another piece of the cigar. "And then you're worried about a cat you keep claiming you're taking to the pound. She had two beautiful babies, by the way. One's gray and white, the other looks just like its mama." He patted Reid on the back. "Welcome to the human race, Peters. I'll have you happily married yet."

"Kiss my ass, Sturgeon. Not going to happen." But the words lacked venom. "Now, let's get to work."

Following the sounds of muted police radios and the thickening iron tang of fresh blood, the two detectives strode into Room 214, and stopped dead.

"Hell!" Sturgeon breathed loudly through his mouth for a moment. "I hate it when they look like this."

Reid just stood and stared.

Sturgeon rounded on the young uniform standing just inside the door. "Where's the rest of it?"

The kid was a delicate shade of yellow-green. He pointed toward the bathroom, where two other uniformed backs could be seen hunched over a bathtub that might've been white before the blood washed it red. "In there."

A flashbulb lit the scene in brilliant white for a nanosecond, making the dark blood gleam against blue-white flesh.

Sturgeon nodded and stepped in that direction. "Peters? You coming?"

The question snapped Reid from his trance. He yanked the squawking radio from the rookie's belt. "Dispatch? Call Patriot and have them send someone to five Old North Road. Tell them to sit tight until I get there."

"Peters? Peters, damn it. What's wrong?" Sturgeon's voice seemed to be coming from a long way away, and Reid didn't answer as he spun on his heel and sprinted for the door.

He felt the dead hooker's eyes following him from the center of the bed, where her decapitated head had been carefully placed next to a row of pistachios that spelled out Last Warning.

Stephanie!

WHEN THE FURIOUS knocking began, Steph wasn't surprised. She had figured Peters would be back when he got the 'message' the voice had threatened. What surprised her was the mix of anticipation and dread that shivered through her. Anticipation because she could share some of the burden. Dread because she'd have to take all of the blame. Own up to her lies.

Blam, blam, blam! "Stephanie! Let me in right now." She could hear him clearly through the heavy door, so he must be yelling at the top of his lungs.

The tension coiled tighter and she went to open the door, wishing she'd let Jilly go when Mortimer had come for Maureen. But she had wanted a few more quiet minutes with her daughter, and Jilly had wanted to stay. The knocking resumed and she grimaced. So much for quiet.

Jilly cooed and waved her hands. Though she usually hated strangers, she'd taken to child-wary Peters right away.

Steph knew the feeling. She hoped he didn't hate her after she confessed what she'd almost done with the DNA results. But that didn't really matter, because he was sure to hate her after she asked him to lose the evidence. Permanently.

"Stephanie? Open up, or I'm breaking the door down."

She wasn't surprised by the cold, angry face that greeted her, but she was startled by the phalanx of cops at his back.

Oh God, she thought. *What's happened now?*

"Inside," Peters snapped at the others. "Check the place top to bottom, and if you miss anything I'll kill you, then give you to your chief. Got it?"

"But sir, we don't have a—"

"I don't care. Do it." His voice was cold. Clipped. Nothing like the sexy grumble she'd heard the night before, after they'd kissed. *You can call me Reid.*

"Reid," she began as a new spurt of terror wrapped itself around her heart. "What's wrong? What happened?"

But the smell of blood and the feel of death hung about him like a shroud and told her that the prayers were useless. Someone had been hurt.

A message.

"In the kitchen," he snapped. His fingers bit into her upper arm much as they had done the night before but with different intent. He half led, half dragged her into the kitchen and shoved her into a chair next to the one where Jilly was eating a banana.

"Reid? Detective Peters! What's happened? What's wrong?"

He loomed over her. She'd known he topped her by almost a foot, but she hadn't before grasped just how physically, elementally *huge* he was. His shoulders were incredibly broad, and she could see the muscles of his upper arms shift and slide beneath his shirt as he grabbed her again, holding her as though he was afraid she might escape.

"Damn it, Stephanie!" Reid yelled, shaking her roughly. "What have you gotten yourself into?" His roar vibrated in the room, echoed by a quiet whimper from Jilly.

He froze.

Steph lurched to her feet and scooped Jilly up, hating the fear in her daughter's eyes. Hating that she'd helped put it there. Hating that her own past misjudgments had taught the child what fear felt like. "Shh, baby. It'll be okay."

She petted Jilly until the child's lower lip stopped trembling, then turned to Peters.

And was surprised to find him most of the way across the room. His face was blank. Cold. "Detective?"

He opened his hands and flexed his fingers once, twice. Then he said, "Detective Sturgeon and I need to see you down at Chinatown Station. Leave the child with Mortimer."

He turned on his heel and left the Patriot cops rifling through her home, finding nothing.

The iron-clad door slammed behind him.

AN HOUR LATER, Reid leaned back against the clammy wall outside the interrogation room and closed his eyes while the anger battered at him, though gentler than it had been that morning. He didn't want to go in there. Didn't want to face the fact that he had acted like the one man he'd sworn never to emulate. And that he'd scared the hell out of Stephanie and Jilly both.

He'd lost control of the rage in a way he'd sworn never to do. The way his father used to.

The memory came clearly, though it was more than twenty-five years old.

"Can't a man come home after a long night shift and expect to find his breakfast ready?" Bronson Peters had slapped the mug of cooling coffee off the table and watched it explode against the cheap, scarred cabinet like a bomb. "And what is this crap?" A plate of eggs followed the mug down to the floor.

In memory, Reid felt his thin, ten-year-old body slide slowly from the kitchen chair and edge toward the door. His mother, who'd been singing along with the radio just minutes before, crouched down and began to clean up the mess while her husband towered over her.

But his father had cop's eyes. Quick eyes. The pale-blue lasers caught his son sneaking out of the room. "You there. Boy! Where do you think you're going?"

His hands were already on his heavy, black belt— the one with all the pouches and buckles that made it whistle through the air and sting like fire.

"What's this I hear about you breaking old man Sykes's window?"

It had happened three weeks before, and Reid had already bought a new pane of glass with his own money and helped their neighbor install it. Then he'd mowed Sykes's lawn, the old man had returned Reid's escaped baseball and they'd called it even. Not that any of that would matter to Reid's father.

His mother had stepped between them and laid a pale, narrow hand on her husband's arm. "Bronson, please—"

He tossed the belt aside and raised his hand. "How many times do I have to tell you not to interfere, woman?" He took another step toward her and she backed away, cowering down against the blows that always followed. "And look at this place, it's a mess. Can't you do anything right?"

The words had echoed in the tiny kitchen as Reid's bellows had done just that morning. And the small boy's fear mirrored that of a dark-eyed child who had already seen too much.

"Damn it!" Reid pushed away from the wall with a vicious shove, and almost caromed into his partner, who was carrying a pair of coffees from the shop down the street.

Sturgeon held one out as though he was offering food to a starving animal and wasn't sure whether he'd be mauled in thanks or not. "What's up?"

Reid took the cup and knocked half of it back before he answered, welcoming the pain of a scalded tongue. "Stephanie Alberts is in there," he nodded at the closed door. "I want to know what she knows about the dead hooker, and I want to know if it has anything to do with Makepeace."

Reid had already told his partner everything. Well, everything except about how it had felt to hold Stephanie in his arms and slide his tongue along hers. How it had felt to touch her cheek in the darkness and fall asleep with her daughter in his lap.

Those were things Sturgeon didn't need to know and Reid couldn't afford to think of.

"So why are you out here and not in there?" the other detective asked.

"I was waiting for you. I want you to question her."

Sturgeon cocked his head. "Why?"

"Because…" Because I scared the hell out of her and her daughter. Because I sounded like the old man. "Because I confronted Stephanie this morning and came on too strong. I think she'd rather talk to you."

Sturgeon wasn't stupid. He offered Reid a peppermint. "What happened?"

Reid stared at the candy. "I went straight to Stephanie's house in Patriot after we saw the hooker."

"Honey Moreplease." Sturgeon supplied the name. The two made it a point to use victims' names as often as possible.

"Yeah, and I'm sure that's on her birth certificate, too," Reid added, knowing that he'd heard the name before. He'd probably run her in when he'd been on patrol. It made the murder more personal somehow. "Anyway, I left the hotel—" with the stench of death in his nostrils and the fear in his heart that Stephanie, Jilly and Maureen were already dead "—and went to her house. I escorted Miss Alberts to the kitchen." He could still feel how far his fingers had pressed into her flesh. She'd probably bruise. "And, well…let's say I wasn't very tactful. It brought back…memories that I'm not very proud of. Things I never wanted to be or do."

"Oh." Sturgeon's single word held a wealth of understanding. More than Reid really wanted. Sturgeon had been a rookie the year Bronson had died. "Peters, your old man was a tough cop in a time that demanded toughness."

Reid glanced over at the door and wished he'd gone in before his partner arrived. Sturgeon meant well, but he'd heard it too many times over the years already. *Your father needs to be that way. He has an important job,* his mother had told him time and again until he wasn't sure which one of them she was trying to convince.

"Yeah, I know. He was a good cop." Reid reached for the interrogation-room door.

"Perhaps," Sturgeon said from behind him. "But you're a better man."

If anything, that made Reid feel worse. If he'd been a better man that morning, he wouldn't have put that look in the little girl's eyes.

He turned the doorknob. "You ready?" When Sturgeon nodded, Reid flashed him a sick-feeling grin. "Okay, you be the good cop." He glanced at his knuckles, which felt swollen and bruised though he hadn't hit a thing. "And I'll be the bad one."

STEPHANIE GLANCED UP as Detective Sturgeon entered the sparse white room that might have intimidated her if she wasn't already at the end of her rope. Reid was on his heels and she could see the lines of temper tight across his forehead. His shoulders were tense, and he wouldn't look her in the eye. She wondered what had happened in Chinatown. Why he'd left her house so abruptly that morning. What it all meant for her and Jilly.

Lose the samples.

The voice had to know who'd raped the little girl.

He'd probably done it himself. Steph shivered, though the little room was warm enough. She wished she'd given in and let Maureen come along, but she knew Jilly and her aunt were safer with Mortimer.

"Miss Alberts." Sturgeon offered her a peppermint, and when she declined, unwrapped it for himself. Stephanie took the moment to look at Reid, who was leaning against the wall at Sturgeon's back. He was glowering at a section of mirrored glass and she wondered whether there was someone on the other side, watching them.

Watching her.

"I'm very sorry to hear about the vandalism at your home last night," Sturgeon began. "Are your aunt and daughter okay?"

Steph cut him a glance. Last night? She'd assumed this was about the Makepeace DNA. About the "message" Reid was supposed to have received. If it wasn't…maybe she still had a chance to "lose" the samples and keep Reid out of it before the voice pulled him in.

The message from Jilly's bed had haunted her dreams and her waking hours. *Do it.* Lose the evidence or find your daughter's head here the next time.

She had no choice.

"Last night?" she repeated with all the cute innocence she could muster, which wasn't much, considering how guilty she felt about lying to Peters. "Well…I went upstairs to put Jilly to bed, and when we got to her room I saw that someone had been in it…''

After a half hour or so, Sturgeon turned to his partner, who was still leaning up against the wall. ''Will you go get us something to drink, please?''

While Reid was gone—and Stephanie felt his absence acutely—Sturgeon led her back over the previous afternoon and evening, and asked a few questions about Jilly's disappearance the day before that. She answered numbly, trying to see into the future and know what was the right path to take.

Tell them? Don't tell them? What would protect Jilly best? Steph had trusted the wrong man before and had almost lost her life. She couldn't afford to choose wrongly again.

Reid returned with the drinks and sat for the first time since the meeting had begun, choosing the chair to Steph's left and placing a bulging envelope on the table. Even looking at Sturgeon, she could feel Reid's presence like a pulse of energy along the left side of her face. She could feel him staring at her, and a secret, guilty thrill rustled inside her when he shifted and his bare forearm brushed against hers.

''Do you have any idea what the words meant? Why did the intruder spell out *Do It* on your daughter's bed?''

Steph shook her head at Sturgeon's question. ''Honestly, I have no idea, Detective.'' She'd never been less honest in her life, but kept the image of her daughter's face firmly in her mind.

She had to protect her family at all costs.

Peters fidgeted with the thick envelope and she wondered what was inside.

"Are you sure you have no idea?" It wasn't the first time Sturgeon had repeated a question, and she had been careful to keep her answers consistent each time.

She sipped from the cup in front of her and paused, surprised. It was hot chocolate. She glanced over and a trickle of warmth stole through her.

"Miss Alberts?" Sturgeon prompted.

"No," she answered. "I don't have any idea why someone might want to write *Do It* on my daughter's bed in broken model horse legs." She shuddered. The legs had been particularly macabre, which she supposed had been the point. "Why? Did you find something?" *Did you get a phone call?* she wanted to ask Reid. *Have you checked your messages and gotten one from a voice that makes you think of death?*

Has the voice told you what you're supposed to do?

"Yes. We found something." Steph jumped slightly when Peters spoke close beside her. His voice was hard and unyielding. A muscle pulsed at his jaw and she wondered how she could be so afraid and so drawn at the same time. The voice on the phone frightened her. The man inside the cop made her want to trust. "And you're going to tell us what you know about it."

He upended the envelope and shook the photographs out and all thoughts of trust and passion fled.

Her stomach clenched as the glossy enlargements slithered across the table, a lurid cascade of white tile and pink water. White flesh and red slashes.

Stephanie's world tilted on its axis. Bile pressed at the back of her throat and she swallowed a scream until it sat, thick and leaden in her stomach.

Red lipstick on a white face. Garish red hair spilling across a pale bedspread, clashing with pink-dyed pistachio words.

Last Warning.

"Oh God!" She stood up and the chair clattered to the floor behind her. She clapped both hands to her mouth to keep the curses and the tears and the screams and her breakfast from rushing out in one huge geyser of horror.

The dead woman's eyes stared at her. The mouth screamed silently.

Her fault. *A message.* If she'd switched the DNA right away, this wouldn't have happened. The voice would have been satisfied.

She staggered back, away from the photos. Away from Peters, who grabbed a photograph of the woman's staring eyes, of the way her neck seemed to end at the bedspread, her life marked by nothing more than a dark stain beneath. He thrust it toward Steph. "Her name was Honey. Got that? Honey." He shoved the photo closer and his quiet voice was louder than his shout had been that morning. "Tell us what you know about the messages."

She shuddered and felt a single tear slide down her cheek.

"Detective Peters," Sturgeon snapped. "That's enough."

Reid glared at him. "She's lying. Don't you see that?" He grabbed another photograph and turned back to Stephanie. Showed her the headless body sprawled in the bathtub. "Now tell me! What does *Do It* mean? What about *Last Warning*?" He shook the photograph. "What if this was your aunt? What if it was Jilly?"

She saw it then. Saw Maureen's eyes looking up at her in mute appeal. Saw a child's body tossed carelessly into an old claw-footed bathtub. Saw the blood, heard the screams.

And she broke.

"That's just it!" She slapped the photograph from his hand and swiped the rest from the table. They fluttered to the floor and lay there, weeping and bloody like the young woman they showed. "Don't you get it? He took Jilly. He said he'd send her back in pieces if I told. He said he'd take Maureen, too."

An unnatural calm descended over her like the sudden silence in the interrogation room, and she nodded at Reid. "He saw you at my house last night...hell, maybe he even saw you at the lab earlier. Either way, he decided you were in this with me. He called just after you left and said he'd sent you a message."

"Son of a—" Reid shot to his feet and began pacing, taking a wide berth around the sloppy pile of crime scene photographs. She could tell he was furious, though she wasn't sure whether he was mad at her or the voice on the phone. "What about *Do It*. What does he want you to do?"

She dropped her face into her hands, because it was simpler than looking at either of the men. Simpler than facing her own choices. "He wanted me to falsify evidence. I was supposed to make sure the results of the Makepeace DNA test came back positive. If I didn't, he said the next time he takes Jilly I'll get her back in pieces."

Reid cursed again and came to a stop, resting his forehead against the privacy window. "And now? What does he want now?" His words echoed strangely off the tinted glass.

"Now he wants us to lose the evidence. If we don't, he says my family and I will die." All three of them looked down at the crime scene photographs, but Steph was the one who said it. "I think he'll do it, too."

Neither of the detectives contradicted her and Steph put her head on her folded arms, trying to block out the memories. The fears. She thought herself too scared for tears. Then she felt Reid's hand on her shoulder and she discovered she wasn't, after all, too scared to cry.

HE HELD Stephanie and cursed himself for her sobs. That it was his job to break the witness and get to the truth was immaterial. That the truth was the only thing that would keep Jilly and Maureen safe was beside the point. The point was that Reid had done it. He'd terrorized her until she broke.

And he hated the fact.

He glanced down at the scattered photos and felt Sturgeon's disapproval like a knife. He knew the older man would have vetoed his plan with the photos in a heartbeat, so he hadn't told him. But he'd seen no other way to crack through that brittle, protective layer that Stephanie hid behind when she lied.

Now, looking at the fragile curve of her neck and feeling the hot tears soak through his shirt, he wished there had been another way. Any other way.

After a long moment, Stephanie quieted and pushed away. Without looking up, she excused herself for the ladies' room and the men watched her leave. Heard the door click behind her.

When she was gone, Reid glanced from the photos to his partner and asked the question they'd both ducked from their superior. "Serial?"

Though there hadn't been any computer hits on similar decapitations, the staged scene smacked of a serial killer. The very thought of such a monster in his own backyard—hell, in Stephanie's house— made Reid want to punch something. Made him want to yell and curse and rage against it all, smashing at anything that got in his way.

But no. That was the old man's way of dealing with things. Instead, Reid held out a hand. "Give me a mint."

Sturgeon complied and crunched a fresh candy of his own. "He's working up to it, maybe. First the teddy bear, then the hooker..." He didn't finish. He didn't need to.

"The rapes had been escalating," Reid observed. It hadn't been released to the papers, but Mae Wong's rape was the sixth in a loosely connected string. "They'd been getting nastier and closer together. He might've made the jump."

Sturgeon shook his head. "From raping a little girl to killing a hooker? Doesn't feel right. Besides, remember that Mae Wong's rape didn't fit so well with the others."

Reid nodded. It had been the only one with DNA left behind, and there were other telling dissimilarities. Though it had superficially matched the other incidents, it *felt* different. He tried a theory on for size. "So maybe Mae Wong isn't part of the pattern. Maybe the same perp did the earlier streetwalker rapes and Honey Moreplease, but not the little girl."

"That would work," agreed Sturgeon, "But we have a connection between Mae Wong and Honey Moreplease through Stephanie. It stands to reason they're all the same guy."

Reid scowled. "Stands to reason, maybe, but I don't like it. The pattern doesn't fit yet."

The door opened quietly, and Stephanie came back in, looking pale and tired. Reid felt his heart stutter in his chest and wanted nothing more than to take her away from all the ugliness and soothe the fears away.

Can't think that way, he told himself. *She's a job, nothing more.*

Because his instincts had been right. She was in

real danger and he couldn't afford to be distracted right now. It could mean Jilly's life. Stephanie's life.

So instead of reaching for Stephanie as he wanted to, Reid gestured her to a chair. "We have a few more questions we'd like to ask you."

And after that, they would make a plan. One thing was for sure, though. He had no intention of letting Stephanie out of his sight until this was all over.

Whether she liked it or not.

Chapter Six

"What the hell's going on?" Molly asked with her typical lack of diplomacy when Stephanie and Peters got to the lab later that morning. "Why are you late and why is Detective Peters here? Is everything okay with Jilly?"

"Jilly's safe with Aunt Maureen." Steph could answer that one truthfully, and only fibbed a little when she added, "And I'm helping the detective with a rush job." She jerked her head back toward the distinctive shape of the evidence kit in his hands.

"Oh. Ick." Molly stepped back, as Steph had known she would. "Thought you guys had police labs for that sort of stuff. Don't leave it on my desk, okay?"

"Over there," Steph waved Peters over to her bench while she grabbed a fresh lab coat. She thought she saw his eyes flash when she pulled the starched white cotton from its hanger, but that had to be an illusion. Ever since they'd left the station he'd been on automatic pilot, barely responsive to her feeble attempts at conversation.

Which was fine. She wasn't feeling chatty either. She'd just thought conversation would keep her from screaming. Her head was pounding in a relentless beat and she was wound so tightly she feared a single touch would shatter her into a thousand pieces.

The detectives had agreed that likely her "voice" had either raped Mae Wong, or knew who had. Makepeace's arrest and the DNA evidence had been publicized enough that the voice had decided to take advantage of the arrest, knowing that Makepeace's conviction would end the search for the serial rapist.

But if it wasn't Makepeace, then who was it?

"Let's get on with it," said Peters, propping Honey Moreplease's evidence on Steph's desk. "First we want to know if Mae Wong and Honey Moreplease were attacked by the same man."

Steph knew he didn't expect the samples to match. He'd said the patterns were too different between the two, but it was an angle they needed to work. Besides, once the second rape kit was processed, they'd have the DNA markers for searching the federal and local DNA databases, which was their real goal.

They weren't going to "lose" the samples as the voice had demanded. They were going to use them to solve the crimes.

And they would hope to God they could keep Jilly and Maureen safe in the process. That was Peters's job. Hers was to process the DNA evidence.

Steph squared her shoulders, donned her lab coat, and prepared to get to work.

Of course Jared had picked up the wrong size coat

again and she had to roll up the cuffs. On a normal day, it would've sent her across the floor to holler at him in person. Today she was horrified to feel tears prickle in her eyes.

"Damn it." She turned away from Reid on the pretext of fussing with a rack of solvents that didn't need to be fussed with, and pressed a hand to her eyes. She would not cry.

She should have told him yesterday. She'd been stupid to believe she was protecting Jilly with her silence. She pressed harder against her eyes, damning the tears that leaked through, as her mind coughed up a remembered image.

A woman's head in the center of a tacky bed-spread. A dark stain beneath.

"Stephanie?" The touch on her shoulder startled her and she jerked away.

The detective stood near where she'd just been, his hand hovering in midair. An expression that might have been pain flickered briefly in his eyes before he let the hand drop.

"I'm—" Sorry, she wanted to say. But she didn't have the right. She'd been lying to him almost from the first. She didn't deserve his forgiveness, and the knowledge hurt more than it should have. She'd been doing what she needed to do to protect Jilly and Aunt Maureen, and in a crazy way even Detective Peters himself, though he'd never thank her for it.

So why did it feel as though she'd been utterly, completely wrong?

Because a woman was dead, she answered herself, and looked at the kit on her lab bench.

"Rape kit's not processing itself, you know," Peters observed mildly, stepping away from her. "You want some help?"

"No." Steph blew out a big breath, snapped on a pair of sterile gloves, and carried the kit to a negatively pressured fume hood that would help to protect the samples from cross-contamination by other DNA stocks. She wiped the area down carefully, though she'd cleaned it herself the night before, and got to work, removing the tubes and swabs from their compartments and keeping careful note of serial numbers and sources. No semen had been found, but the hand that had hung outside the half-filled bathtub had had skin under its fingernails. "I've got it from here, and the whole thing will take most of the day to run. I've got to extract the DNA and amplify the markers we're checking before I can run them on any gels. You can come back later tonight if you want. I should have some preliminary results by then."

But Peters shook his head and settled back in the tall swivel chair at her bench. "I think I'll stick with you for the day, okay?"

It was anything but okay in Stephanie's book. She didn't want him there, didn't want to feel his presence humming along her nerve endings and didn't want to brush up against him when she reached for reagents. She especially didn't want to have to see the look of betrayal in his eyes and know that he wasn't sticking around because he enjoyed her company.

He was staying because he didn't trust her not to mess with the results. And she couldn't blame him.

Wincing, she directed a thin stream of DNA-extracting solution toward the clean test tube she'd used to hold the swab labeled LF for left-hand fingernails.

Instantly, Honey's face filled her mind again.

"Something wrong?"

Damn the man. He must be watching her like a hawk, waiting for her to make a wrong move. Steph shook her head and refused to move away from the fume hood when Peters stepped closer. "Stay back," she snapped, "unless you're planning on breathing on the evidence."

It was actually fairly hard to contaminate DNA, but he didn't have to know that. Having him in the building was distracting enough without him hovering over her shoulder and breathing on the sensitive spot at the back of her neck she hadn't even known existed. He jumped back and repeated the question from a distance.

Her hands trembled slightly as she swirled the light-green liquid around inside the tube. "Nothing's wrong. And everything." She gestured at the rape kit. "I've never seen the victim before, you know?"

She wished she'd seen a picture of the young woman when her head was still attached to her body. Perhaps that would have dulled the images that kept slashing through her mind. She pictured the naked, headless body in the tub. Pictured the swabs doing their work.

And trembled.

Peters cursed. "This is a bad idea, and probably skirts the edges of legal. Someone else should do this. I'll see if the state lab has room for it."

Steph shook her head. "No way. They're backed up for weeks, that's why you brought the work to Boston General, remember? Besides, I can do it." She *had* to do it. Jilly's safety was at stake.

The detective cursed again, then fell silent as he watched her process all of the samples with ruthlessly steady hands. She could feel the anger and the accusations tumble off him like rain.

But when he spoke, it surprised her, and unaccountably made her angry. "I'm sorry," he said. "I didn't mean to…" He trailed off and she shook her head.

"Of course you 'meant to,'" she snapped, turning to irritation when guilt prodded too deeply. "You meant to shock me with those photos. Horrify me. Make me feel so wracked with guilt that I'd tell you what you wanted to know." She stabbed a pipette full of ethanol into the oral sample and watched the DNA precipitate out of the solution like spun silk. "Well, it worked."

"Stephanie…" He reached out toward her, and Steph had never been so glad for the protection of a lab coat and surgical gloves.

"Don't contaminate the field," she ordered, and he dropped his hand.

Da-da-da-*DUM*! The burble of his cell phone sliced through the tension and she felt her shoulders slump as he looked at her one last time as though she still wasn't getting the point. Then he answered the phone with a bark. "Peters!"

He turned away, and as she spun the samples down to let gravity separate the precipitated DNA strands from the lighter liquid, all she could make out were a string of uh-huh's and muttered expletives.

When he slapped the phone shut, he was scowling even harder. But when she lifted an eyebrow in question, he shook his head. "Nothing."

She wasn't sure whether that meant the call wasn't important or that he wouldn't share the information with her. So she went back to work.

Now that the DNA was stuck to the sides of the plastic tubes, she could dump the spent solution into a waste receptacle. She placed the tubes in a spinning vacuum drier in the hall and set the timer for fifteen minutes.

Snapping her gloves off, she tossed them in the direction of the trash. "I'm going to the fourth floor for a cup of something. You want any?"

Even through his mood, Peters found a ghost of a grin, bringing out the dimple on his left cheek that she hadn't noticed until the moment she'd found him asleep on her daughter's bed. Lust was a hard punch beneath her aching heart, painful and unwelcome.

"I'd love a cup of 'something,'" he answered.

She almost withdrew the invitation, but didn't. The fact that he was angry with her was almost a good thing. He wasn't likely to kiss her again if he was pissed at her. And she didn't think she could handle another kiss right now.

Maybe not ever. Their clinch in her kitchen the night before had been the sort of kiss she'd been waiting her whole life for. It had touched a piece of her that nobody had found before. Not Luis. Not Roger. Nobody.

And he was a cop who didn't like kids. Period.

"Mail call," Terry caroled as they passed him in the front office. The grad student was signing for a flat brown package. "It's for you, Steph. Order something fun?"

She shrugged and headed for the elevator, aware of Peters following close behind. "Probably those new spin columns I'm trying. Just toss it on my desk, okay?"

Terry nodded. "Sure thing."

They rode down to the fourth floor in silence, and Steph found herself acutely aware of Reid's breathing and the way he flexed his fingers as though he wished he was holding something. When they stepped out of the close little car, he touched her arm and she stopped, feeling the contact all the way to her toes.

She turned to him. "Yes?"

"I'm sorry about this morning."

It wasn't what she'd expected. "I thought we already went through this. You wanted to scare me with those photos. It worked. I may never sleep again."

He shook his head. "No. Not the photos. I'm sorry for barging into your house like that and scaring you and your daughter."

"Oh." His outburst had been a minor ripple in the tidal wave of drama she'd been living through the last few days. Apparently he thought it was more. "Why are you sorry for that and not the photos?"

"Showing a witness crime scene photographs is acceptable police work," he replied. "Yelling at a woman and child in their own home is not. I'm sorry for it. It was unprofessional and won't happen again."

She shrugged. "Okay. You're forgiven for yelling. Coffee or tea?" She pushed into the cafeteria and shoved a carry-out cup in his direction.

He didn't take it right away. "That's it?"

She looked at him sideways. "People yell. Kids cry. You get over it—no big deal. You should hear Maureen and Mortimer go at it some days. They really hate each other." Though she wasn't so sure of that any more. The two had arrived at the same time the night before. Coincidence? She wasn't sure.

She continued. "Tell you what. I'll forgive you for yelling at me this morning if you forgive me for lying to you yesterday."

It would take her longer to forgive herself, and an eternity to forget the sight of Honey's sightless brown eyes, but she didn't think she could bear to spend the rest of the day feeling his anger radiating from her bench area.

He shrugged one shoulder, and the dimple put in a quick appearance. "I'm not mad at you."

"Well, you should be. I should've told you about the phone call yesterday. I wasn't thinking straight." She wondered if she ever would again. "But if you're sticking around until this experiment is done, I'd like to declare a truce." She stuck out a hand. "Truce?"

Reid stared at the hand for a moment, and his eyes blazed gold.

Instead of shaking it, he lifted her hand to his lips and pressed a warm, intimate kiss to her knuckles. His eyes flickered to hers and her pulse jumped several notches. "Truce," he breathed across the suddenly sensitive skin, and Steph wondered when she'd become a ball of nerves centered around her first two knuckles.

She yanked her hand away and covered her sudden confusion by jamming her cup beneath a random spigot and filling it to the brim while her heart thundered in her ears.

"Come on, then," she said, spinning and heading back toward the elevator a full five minutes before her timer would start its annoying beep. "Let's get back to work." She wouldn't—*couldn't*—deal with her attraction to Peters right now.

They rode upstairs in a tense silence that was broken only when they walked back through the reception area and saw Molly chatting with a uniformed courier. "You guys are keeping the couriers busy today," Reid commented.

Steph nodded as they walked into the lab. "Looks like it. This is our usual guy. The other package must've been a special delivery." She paused and turned back to Reid as something niggled at her. "But why would Petrie Pharmaceuticals pay for special delivery of spin columns?"

She saw the knowledge in his eyes just as it clicked in her own brain, but it was too late.

With a deceptively mild *whump!* her lab bench exploded in a ball of orange flame and detonating lab chemicals.

Something hard and heavy slammed into Steph, and she found herself face down beneath Terry's bench at the far end of the lab. She couldn't breathe and she couldn't move. But she could hear. The sound of shattering glass and screams made her long to close her eyes and hide. The sound of running feet and slamming doors let her know the others were fleeing.

With good reason. The lab flammables were going up like rockets.

Relatively safe beneath the granite bench, Steph turned her face away from the noise and pressed her cheek against Reid's sleeve, only then realizing that he had pushed her to safety and was covering her with his own body for protection.

Protection. "Jilly! Aunt Maureen!" She struggled and managed to roll over beneath him before he grabbed her and pinned her more securely. She saw a clear liquid rain down on the other side of them as a bottle on Terry's bench shattered.

It could be water. It could be hydrochloric acid. There was no telling.

They were trapped.

"Quit! Stay down, damn it. What's your problem?" They were face to face, only a breath apart and she could see the fierceness in his eyes. Feel the drum of his heart against her breasts.

Feel her nipples crinkle as the heat from the bomb swirled around them and the sound of running feet and breaking glass faded and the whoop-whooping of the fire alarms began.

"Jilly," she whispered almost against his lips. "Maureen. What if he sends them a package too?"

But even through the fear and the Klaxons and the shouts from the outer office, Steph could feel something warm and feminine uncurl within her and reach out to Reid's hard, enduring masculinity.

"Mortimer will keep them safe," he replied, "And the men watching the house." They both knew the police detail hadn't been enough to protect her from Roger the year before. But it seemed enough for the moment, when she was cleanly divided between terror and growing desire for the man who'd saved her yet again.

"Reid," she whispered, though she didn't know what she wanted to say.

It seemed enough. His eyes flashed yellow gold, and when something on the bench above them fell with a crash, they flinched into each other and their lips met.

And held.

There was another explosion, though Steph couldn't tell if it was in the lab or in her heart. The temperature spiked and heat roiled around them, licking along her skin like a lover though they were safe enough a half a room away from the small fire, tangled together beneath the granite-topped bench.

His tongue touched hers and his hand slid down her arm. She could feel the heat from his body sear through the rough cotton of the starched lab coat. The linoleum floor was hard against her back, but she welcomed the pressure when he gathered her closer and closer still, changing the angle of the kiss and dragging her along with him into deeper, darker territories.

He tasted of coffee and let out a groan of sharp frustration that she knew all too well and feared would never be appeased.

She wanted to pull away and scream for the unfairness of it all.

She wanted never to pull away again, but rather to lose herself in the taste of him, the feel of his hard, huge body against her, and the feeling of warm safety that stole through her as he wrapped himself around her as though he would never let go.

Then, over the sound of their breathing and a soft moan that could have belonged to either of them, Steph heard a loud *thunk!* and a growing hiss all around them, as though it was raining in the lab.

Reid stiffened and pulled away, turning his head quickly toward the water flooding down outside their temporary shelter in the large space beneath Terry's desk. ''Sprinklers.'' Still without looking at her, he stood and glanced around at the lab, silent now except for the hissing of the sprinklers and the last few dying flames. Even the alarms had stilled, leaving only the blink of the exit indicators to show that there was a problem. He reached a hand down. ''Come on. Let's get out of here.''

He was right, it was time to leave. The overhead blowers had shut down when the fire alarm was activated, and the air was rapidly filling with the stink of chemicals. Steph pressed her sleeve against her nose and mouth, blinked back tears and scrambled to her feet. But her mind wasn't wholly focused on the smell and the water that rained down around them.

She felt the cool drops hit her hot, flushed skin, and thought of the man beside her.

She wanted more of him. All of him. That was all she could think. Not about the bomb, or the lab, or, God help her, even her daughter, Steph could only think that she wanted Reid Peters. Wanted all of him.

She followed him toward the exit, thinking that the darkroom was on the other side of the outer office, down a short corridor. Her whole body heated as she conjured a picture of the two of them in there, lit only by the dark lights as she untucked his shirt. Let his trousers down just far enough to free the part of him she wanted most. Hitched herself up on the waist-high counter and spread her legs to guide him home—

''Stephanie.'' His voice was as gritty as her throat felt, and she almost exploded right there at the desire in his molten-gold eyes, almost swooned with the need to have him inside her.

"Yes, Reid." Yes to all of it. Any of it. Whatever, whenever, however he wanted it. The sharp bite of spilled chemicals in the air and the steady downpour from the sprinklers made her think of springtime and being in love.

"I can't." She could see the moment he regained control. The moment he shifted from man to cop and shut her out entirely. Shut himself in. "I won't. You're..." He seemed to search for the word. "You're a *victim*. It's not right." He held her eyes for another long moment as they both heard the hubbub of the rescue personnel arrive in the outer office. He whispered, "I'm sorry," but she barely heard.

She heard only the word *victim* crashing around in her brain as he let himself into the outer office.

And left her standing in the rain.

Chapter Seven

An hour later, Reid was still waiting for his system to level off. It hadn't yet. He could still feel her. Still taste her.

It was driving him so crazy, he'd almost asked Sturgeon to stay in the lab and watch her finish the experiment. But he hadn't been able to leave her any more than he'd been able to tell her the real reason he wasn't going to follow up on that wonderful, terrifying, explosive kiss.

No, he hadn't told her about his father, or about the little girl and the rag doll, or about the look of fear he'd seen too often in his mother's eyes, a look that he'd seen again in Stephanie's daughter's eyes when he'd burst into their kitchen in a rage.

Instead, he'd blamed it on the job, which was only part of the reason he could never, ever kiss her again.

"Are you sure they're safe?"

He glanced over at Stephanie, watching as she used a ridiculously thin plastic needle to load blue-dyed DNA into the machine that would separate out the samples from Honey Moreplease's fingernail and

tell them if the DNA matched that taken from
Mae Wong.

"Yeah. They're safe," he answered, knowing she
was thinking of her aunt and daughter. Her own
safety, it seemed, was secondary. Finishing the experiment came first. Ever since she'd followed him
out of the ruined lab, dripping with water and shiv-
ering with shock and cold, Steph had been like a
woman possessed.

The rape kit, paperwork and chemicals that had
been on her desk were a dead loss, but little of the
rest of the lab had been touched, thanks to the fire-
proof cabinet that held the most dangerously flam-
mable solvents. The bomb squad had come and gone,
pronouncing the timer and homemade explosive
crude but effective, and Steph had gotten back to
work. The samples she'd extracted from the rape kit
had been in a drier down the hall, and the DNA from
Mae Wong had been stored in a shielded freezer. So
she'd directed Molly to contact Genie and start the
cleanup of the Watson lab, sent the other employees
home and headed over to the Wellington lab with
only a bare glance for the scorched corner that had
once been her workstation.

She'd hardly looked at him in the two hours since.
Reid was starting to get twitchy from all the silence,
combined with the lingering smell of scorched plastic
from the other side of the hall. It was late at night
and he wasn't sure what came next.

Not a familiar feeling, nor a comfortable one.

"They're fine," he repeated, more to keep the conversation going than from any real conviction.

She squinted at the gel and added another sample. "Why do you think he sent the bomb? He didn't even give us a chance to lose the samples. How could he have known we weren't going to?"

Her unspoken questions lingered between them. *What will he do now? Am I still in danger? Is my family?*

"We're not sure, Stephanie. It's complicated." Confusing. Sturgeon had gone so far as to suggest two perps, one who was threatening her and one who'd planted the bomb. The two MOs didn't jibe with each other any more than Mae's rape and Honey's murder fit the pattern of the earlier rapes. The case was starting to come unglued when it should have been pulling together. It would almost be a relief if the DNA didn't match. Then they'd have evidence to back up their suspicion of a second perp.

"Uncomplicate it for me, okay?" She finished loading the samples and covered the ice bucket with a heavy plastic shield while she plugged the leads into the machine and started the electrical current.

Reid sighed heavily and gave her the bare bones of the theory he and Sturgeon had spent most of the afternoon pounding out as they sat in the far corner of the ruined Watson lab. "Mae Wong's rape wasn't the first this guy pulled off. There were at least five others before that fit the same pattern, but no DNA before her case." Which had always bothered Reid.

The perp had left nothing at the other rapes. Why start with that one? Besides, though the setting and the act had been the same, the others hadn't been children. Why break pattern?

The pattern, or lack thereof, disturbed him. He felt as if they were missing something important. But what?

"Why did you arrest Makepeace?" She was washing her hands now, still not looking at him. But that was fine with Reid, who was caught in a strange twilight between the job and the woman. He feared that if she kissed him now, or even smiled, it would be all over for him. For both of them.

So he concentrated on the job. He knew the job. He could trust it to be there every morning when he woke up, and he could trust himself to do it justice.

He couldn't say the same for Stephanie. Or her daughter.

"Makepeace," he repeated the name to center himself and to keep from reaching for her, "is a slimy weasel who lives in the basement of the Wongs' apartment building and has priors for indecent exposure and sexual misconduct. He had scratches on his face and no alibi." And both Reid and Sturgeon had liked him for the rapes. Damn it.

"There weren't any fingernail scrapings in Mae Wong's kit," Steph observed as she racked and stacked the samples in the radioactive refrigerator. "So she didn't scratch him."

Reid nodded. "And it wasn't his semen. So we're back to square one." He nodded to the machine that was running the DNA samples, ''Plus some forensic evidence. If the DNA from Mae Wong and Honey Moreplease match…''

She finished for him, ''Then we know the voice wanted me to help convict Makepeace so the real rapist would be off the hook.''

''Yeah.'' But it didn't feel right. Reid could swear that Mae and Honey were done by two different perps. The scenes were too different. The level of violence too distinct.

Last Warning. He thought of the pistachio words and ground his teeth. Imagined the sleeve of a white lab coat dangling from the pinkened bathtub and clenched his fists. Thought of what might have happened had Stephanie been at her desk when the mail bomb exploded and cursed out loud.

No way. There was no way he was letting anything happen to her or to her family.

No way in hell.

Reid felt his temperature rise and knew he needed to burn off some steam before he exploded. He glanced over at Steph, who was logging information into the new lab notebook she'd gotten from the storeroom to replace the one that had been incinerated. ''We've got a couple hours before that's done, right?'' he said, indicating the humming machine.

She nodded and he felt his blood burn even hotter when she finally looked at him. He could see his own desires and confusions mirrored in her jade eyes. ''Why?''

''Let's get out of here.'' He felt the familiar

weight of his shoulder holster and knew that he had a better chance of protecting her from the voice on the phone than he did of protecting her from making a huge mistake with a screwed-up cop from the Chinatown precinct. She'd been hurt by a madman who'd used her for access to the lab, and by an ex-husband who'd taken her for everything she was worth. She didn't need another mistake like that. "I need to walk."

Needed to get the hell out of here before he hiked her up on the nearest lab bench and finished what they'd started earlier.

She looked at him through protective eyewear that should have made her look ridiculous. Then she smiled and looked nothing less than beautiful. She pulled the glasses off and shook her curly red hair free. She drew her latex surgical gloves off one at a time, loosening them from the fingertips before stripping them off and tossing them aside.

Reid's mouth went dry when her fingers touched the lapels of her lab coat. Slid the first button free. Then the next, opening a doorway to tantalizing glimpses of the clothing beneath.

Willpower, he told himself, and turned his back on Stephanie while she stripped out of the starched white lab coat. She was a victim. A mother. And she would never belong to him.

He held out a hand without looking. "Let's walk."

Yes, let's walk, he thought. *Before I go insane.*

IT WASN'T UNTIL they reached a seedy little neighborhood amidst a bunch of other seedy little neighborhoods that Steph realized where they'd walked to. His house. She shivered a little as he gestured her up steps that were barely lit by a cracked streetlamp.

"Cold?" His voice came out of the darkness, low and intimate, and Steph felt a sharp tug of wanting. It had been more than three years since a man's voice had spoken to her once the lights were out.

Don't go there, she told herself. *He's already turned you down once today, and besides, your taste in men is atrocious.*

Though she supposed a cop was about as far on the other end of the spectrum from her previous men as it was possible to get, even if he thought of her as nothing more than a victim.

She shook her head, knowing he could see through the shadows. "Not really." But she rubbed her hands across the goose bumps that shivered to attention on her bare arms, though the Chinatown night was warm and wet.

"Let's get you inside, then." He reached past her to unlock the dark-brown door, and his sleeve brushed her breast, causing a thousand needle pricks of sensation to race across her chest and arrow straight to her core. She sucked in a breath and he froze, staring down at the place where they touched.

"Reid, I—"

"No," he interrupted. "My fault. I'm sorry." He glanced at her face, and Steph could see the desire banked behind ruthless cop restraint, and she heard the word echo in her head. *Victim.*

If that was all he saw her as, no wonder he didn't want to be involved. But she'd been a victim twice in her life—once with Luis and again with Roger. She'd be damned if she was going to stand for it a third time. So she straightened up and swept into his house, damning herself for the compulsion that had her memorizing every detail and filling her lungs with his scent.

"It's not much to look at, but it's close to work," he said behind her. "Not nearly as nice as Patriot, as Sturgeon often reminds me."

"It looks…" She stalled, trying to find something nice to say. "Convenient."

There weren't any dishes in the sink, and the counters and tables were neat. He wasn't a slob. But the whole place was *brown*. Drab. Neither loved nor lived in. Even the spider plant in the corner was brown, which couldn't be a good sign as she was almost sure it was made of silk and plastic.

"Come meet She Devil," he invited with a wave into a back room she could only assume was the bedroom, and with a start, Steph remembered the woman he'd been heading home to the night before.

She'd kissed him since then. Twice. And he hadn't kissed like a man involved with another woman.

Then again, neither had her ex-husband.

Reid's voice, husky and intensely sexual, drew her to the bedroom and she hovered at the doorway, feeling half-wronged and half-guilty. He was murmuring soft endearments to the other woman, and it wasn't until she damned herself and leaned closer to catch the words that she heard the response.

Squeaking. And a soft meow.

She stepped the rest of the way into the room and didn't see another woman. She saw Detective Peters's suit jacket tossed across a bed that was neatly made with a brown spread. And she saw the detective himself, shoulder holster strapped in place, kneeling before an open drawer that held a calico cat and a pair of day-old kittens.

He clucked and the little cat answered with a rusty meow. And Stephanie felt her heart lurch and knew she was teetering at the edge of a very steep, very dangerous cliff.

With jagged rocks at the bottom.

She took a physical step back, as though the chasm itself had opened up in the floor of Reid's brown bedroom. His eyes found hers. He held out a hand. ''You like cats?''

''Who doesn't?'' But she stayed where she was and glanced at the bed.

Warm gold gleamed and he cocked an eyebrow. Where a moment before the air had seemed to shimmer with gentleness and new life, now it pulsed with something else.

Something elemental.

He rose and crossed the room to stand before her. She would have backed away, but she was pulled toward him just as surely as she knew she should run. She felt the memory of his kiss on her lips and wanted another. Wanted more.

He glanced from her to the bed and back, and the web of sudden intimacy and her own thoughts made it seem only a little surprising when he asked, ''What about your ex-husband?''

''What about him?'' She leaned closer, wanting his lips on hers. Wanting his arms and his warmth. Wanting the feeling of safety in the middle of so much fear. ''I don't love him anymore. I'm not sure I ever did.'' She'd loved the idea of Luis, the concept of being part of a real family with a mother and a father and a child.

The plan had been sound, but her choice of a mate had been anything but.

Remembering the shame and the hurt cooled her blood a degree. She leaned back and tried to regain her equilibrium. She looked up into Reid's eyes and saw not the molten gold of returned desire, but the cool, shuttered look she associated with *cop*.

He had withdrawn to that place she couldn't enter. But why? She crossed her arms and hugged herself for warmth in the toasty little room. ''It was a long time ago.''

He touched her cheek, but the distance remained in his eyes. ''I'd still like to know what happened.''

Was he asking as a cop or a man? It was a man's question, but a cop's eyes.

''I met Luis in a bar when I was a sophomore in college.'' She shot Reid a glance. She'd edited this story so many times she hardly knew what was truth and what was polite fiction anymore. But if she couldn't give Jilly a proper family, she could at least hide the fact that the little girl's father was a criminal. If Reid cared enough to find out the rest, he would. "We dated for a few months, married and I got pregnant with Jilly."

Not necessarily in that order, but she'd been young and Luis had said all the right things. She shrugged as though it hadn't mattered, though it had. "It didn't work out and we divorced. Jilly doesn't see him. I don't see him. End of story."

"Is it?" The cop look had taken over Reid's eyes and he took a step away. He retrieved his suit jacket and drew it over his holster, smoothing the lapels as though he needed to do something, anything with his hands. "What about the part where he took all your money and hopped a plane bound for Antigua?" The knowledge was in his eyes. Steph could practically see the word *victim* spelled out in his brain. He'd known all along, she realized. He knew about Luis. He knew about Roger. He knew she was a failure at the man-woman thing.

Reid continued. "And you left out the part where he was arrested at customs on two year-old embezzlement charges and the fact that he's in county lockup right now and you never got your money back. Did those little details just slip your mind?"

Steph felt a blush rise, but surprisingly, anger was close behind. Her voice rose a notch and the bite of irritation felt better than the fear. "No, that information didn't 'slip my mind,' Peters. I decided it wasn't your business."

"Wrong!" the detective barked. And he was

clearly Detective Peters now, not Reid. "If protecting you and your daughter is my responsibility then it's absolutely my business. Your ex is in jail. Didn't you ever stop to think that he might be involved in this?"

"Of course I did," Steph snapped. "And I can't see any connection. Besides, if you've already investigated him enough to know he's in jail—and have presumably cleared him in this case—then why'd you ask me about him in the first place? You already know he got me pregnant, took my inheritance and left me with a pile of bills. Why bother asking?"

Peters scowled and jammed a few items in an overnight bag. "I wanted to see what you'd say."

I wanted to see if you'd lie.

The unspoken words echoed between them like a sigh and Steph felt her shoulders slump. As she followed him out the front door into the humid funk of Chinatown, she muttered, "These things that you call lies, Detective, I call protecting my daughter."

Only a slight stiffening of the broad shoulders in front of her acknowledged a direct hit.

SHE HAD LIED to him. Again. That it had been a sin of omission didn't make it any better in Reid's mind. She still didn't trust him. And he still wanted her.

Reid scowled as he watched her remove a film cassette from the lab freezer and wished it could be different. Wished they could have dated casually the year before and that they'd grown tired of each other. It would be easier to remember her fondly than to exist in this perpetually half-aroused state of alternating between wanting to strangle her and wanting to strip her bare beneath the starchy lab coat and pin her to the nearest desk.

Madness.

Then his phone rang and images of naked redheads gave way to images of death and dismemberment. Tears and trials. His job. His life.

A life with no place for a woman. He sighed and answered, "Peters."

Sturgeon wasted no time. "They popped Makepeace loose an hour ago. No reason to hold the slimy little weasel if the DNA didn't match, and I couldn't stall the paperwork any longer. Sorry."

Reid muttered a curse. That meant whoever had threatened Stephanie would know they were once again looking for Mae Wong's rapist. He swore again, and saw her eyes go round. He shook his head and mouthed *everything's fine,* but he could see she didn't believe it.

And really, why should she? It was a lie.

"Anything else on your end?" he asked Sturgeon, and got a grunt in reply.

"Nope. I'm backtracking over all the stuff we did to come up with Makepeace as a suspect in Mae Wong's rape, but it's pretty cold. That was almost six months ago now. I pulled Dodd and Chang in on the Moreplease case..." Sturgeon's voice barely quivered over the ridiculous name, but Reid imagined it had caused a stir back at Chinatown station. "But it's up to forensics now. We could use a few good fibers or a shoeprint on this one if your Miss Alberts can't do anything with the DNA.''

"We'll see about that in a few minutes," Reid glanced at "his" Miss Alberts and felt a wistful tug. "I'll call you when I have something."

IT WAS CLOSE to midnight when the film was ready for processing, but Stephanie wasn't tired. She was wired and edgy as she avoided looking toward Genie's side of the thirteenth floor. She couldn't think of that now. Wouldn't.

Jilly and Maureen were safe—she'd called several times to be sure of it—and it was time to develop the film that would tell them once and for all whether the voice on the phone had wanted to convict Makepeace because he'd done the crime himself. Then, once they were sure they had the proper DNA, they would be able to scan it into the federal and local databases and see what happened.

Maybe they'd get lucky and a name would pop up and it would all be over.

Stephanie darted a glance at Reid, thinking that once it was over she'd go back to imagined sightings of him across Kneeland Street. The idea made her sadder than it should have, but ever since that moment earlier when she would have given him everything and asked for nothing in return, she had rebuilt most of her defenses. He'd been right to pull away from her. She might not be a victim in her own mind, but she was a mother, and he'd made it plain he wasn't the family type.

She thought wistfully of the look on his face as he knelt beside the kittens, then mentally kicked herself. He'd made no bones about it. He didn't want to be involved with her. So she'd depend on him to keep her safe for now and ask nothing more from him.

She wouldn't ask for something he couldn't give.

"All set to develop the film?" He must have dozed for a moment, because his voice was husky with sleep and his hair was slightly mussed. Steph had to stop herself from smoothing it down. Instead she mustered a nod. "All set. I'm going to take it to the developer room now."

He straightened with a wince and she wondered if he'd been hit by something during the explosion. He hadn't said anything, but that didn't mean he wasn't hurting. But he forestalled her question by announcing, "I'll go in with you. I want to see it the moment it's done."

He wanted to go into the darkroom. With her. The thought brought a shiver, not of fear, but of excitement. Once, Steph had asked Genie whether she was afraid of the little room, and had been treated to a sly-eyed wink. Since then, she'd noticed the newlywed lab leaders sneak into the darkroom together on more than one occasion and emerge looking decidedly satisfied.

Now, Steph imagined Reid and her in the room together, surrounded by warm darkness and waist-high counters. A red flush climbed her cheeks. "You can't come into the developer room with me."

"Why not? You aren't going to switch the results on me, are you?" He was only half-kidding.

She shook her head. "Absolutely not. It's just…" Too small." Too full of possibilities.

Those golden eyes saw too much. He turned away. "Never mind. I'll wait in the hall. Ready?"

Ready or not, she slid through the revolving doors and fed the cool film into the X-ray developer. Moments later, she was back outside in the white, safe hallway that didn't have a single sexy-looking counter in it.

But it did have a sexy-looking detective in it, frowning as he held up the developed gel. "Does this say what I think it says?"

She glanced at the patterns and nodded. "I'll have to run it through the scanner to be a hundred-percent sure, but it looks like a match to me."

They stood shoulder to shoulder and looked at the black bars that shadowed the silver-gray film. Reid swore quietly, before handing the data to her and rubbing his hands on his thighs to wipe away the last of the emulsion.

"It's him," she said unnecessarily.

He nodded. "Yeah. It's him. Now we just have to figure out who the hell *he* is."

Chapter Eight

It was silly for her to feel let down by the results, Steph thought a few minutes later as she moved through the floor, shutting the equipment down for the night. She'd been in science long enough to know that most experiments raised more questions than they answered. But still, some small part of her had hoped the black bars on the X-ray film would spell out "Joe Schmo Is *Guilty!*" or some such nonsense.

Instead, all it had proved was that the same man had raped Mae Wong and killed Honey Moreplease, and Steph had the distinct impression that the knowledge bothered Reid.

She'd watched enough forensics programs on TV to know that serial rapists, like serial killers, had patterns that rarely changed. So why had the same man raped a five-year-old child, then killed a thirty-something prostitute? And what about the other rapes she'd heard Reid and Sturgeon talking about? Those victims had been older teens, and there had been no DNA left behind. No hair, no semen. And then there was the mail bomb. It had been addressed to her and timed to detonate after delivery. But what had been its purpose—to hurt her? To destroy the DNA evidence? It had done neither.

Was the very lack of pattern his pattern? It didn't make any sense, and Steph hated the uncertainty. She shut down the last of the machines and shivered at the sudden silence in the Wellington lab, and at the lingering smell of fire from the other side of the building. Her purse had survived the conflagration because it had been in the computer room, but her lightweight jacket had been reduced to ashes.

No. She wouldn't think of that now. Wouldn't think of how close she'd come to being blown to kingdom come. Wouldn't think of Maureen being forced to raise yet another generation's orphan.

"Ready?" Reid's voice broke the silence and Steph shivered again at the sliver of heat that pierced her when he stepped near and slipped his suit jacket over her shoulders.

She tried not to turn her nose into the collar of his jacket, nodding instead. "Ready."

They called the elevator in silence and she was acutely aware of the overnight bag he carried in one hand. He had packed a change of clothes at his place and neither of them had talked about the fact that he would stay with her another night.

But the knowledge and the possibilities crackled around them like electricity as they walked to the Jazz Cat, the blues club on the Patriot/Chinatown line that Mortimer owned.

They were to meet Maureen and Jilly there, as

Mortimer hadn't been able to get anyone to cover for him on short notice. As far as Steph was concerned, Jilly slept hard enough that a few hours at a jazz club would be fine if it meant she was safely surrounded by watchful people.

Mortimer had assured them that he'd see to it personally. He was taking his protection of Maureen and Jilly very, very seriously, and if Steph tried to find an up side to the last few days, perhaps enforced togetherness would put an end to the long, pitched saxophone feud between Maureen and Mortimer.

They walked through the night, silent as the darkness around them. Steph noticed that Reid kept the corner of his eye on the shadows across the street as they turned into a narrow alley. The shadows didn't move, at least not that she could see.

''Is someone out there?'' she whispered.

''You're safe with me,'' he answered, which wasn't really an answer, and Stephanie almost snorted.

On one level, she trusted Reid to keep her as safe as he possibly could. But on another level she was in the deepest danger she'd ever known, and it was becoming increasingly obvious that her heart was intent on sending her along a fast track to disaster.

Why can't I fall for a guy who isn't a criminal, likes kids and likes me? Is that so much to ask? She wasn't sure if she asked the question to take her mind off the shadow she felt slipping from parked cars to deserted doorways, but it was unanswerable just the same and she scowled as they marched through some of the seediest parts of seedy neighborhoods in order to reach the club. She'd never have walked through here alone during the day, never mind at night. But Reid was right. At least in this instance, she was safe with him. He would protect her.

But would it be enough? There was no way to tell. She just prayed they would get a hit off one of the databases. It was her fondest wish that once she fed the DNA results into the federal database, it would burp out a name. Perhaps even an address.

It could all be over the next day.

"We're here," Reid said unnecessarily, holding open the door to Mortimer's club. Happy laughter, light and the smooth slide of saxophone danced out into the night, seeming foreign to Stephanie. Inside the bar, people were drinking, flirting and falling in love as though there wasn't someone out there in the darkness waiting for her to be alone.

She shivered. Reid took a step toward her, but she shook her head and held him off. "I'm okay." She would have to be. She slid out of his jacket and handed it to him with a murmur of thanks and the thought that she might never get his scent out of her head now. She took a deep breath of clean air, nodded and dove into the club with Reid at her heels.

They found Maureen at a little round table off to one side of the wide wooden stage, where a twist of the speakers and a small alcove provided a quiet nook away from the press of bodies and noise. Jilly was fast asleep, wrapped in a blanket and cushioned on a pile of coats.

"You're here," Maureen shot to her feet and grabbed Steph in a fierce hug that took them both by surprise. "I was worried."

"I'm fine, Aunt Maureen." Steph hadn't told her aunt about the bomb. She and Reid had agreed they would hold a council of war that evening. She bent to press a kiss to her daughter's cheek, inhaling the little-girl scent and feeling the band around her heart loosen a little. "Is everything okay here?"

"Sure, if you like being chained to a jazz club for hours at a time." Maureen frowned and waved her hand at the stage, where Mortimer and several other men of various ages and colors slid into a sexy, bluesy number that Steph vaguely recognized. Mortimer's eyes flickered over to the table in the corner, and he winked at Stephanie.

Or perhaps Maureen.

"You like jazz," she reminded her aunt. "You made me listen to all those records over and over when I was a child, and when I took up the clarinet—"

Reid interrupted the mini trip down memory lane. "Sorry, ladies, but it's time to be going. Do you want me to carry the kid?"

"I've got her." Stephanie scooped Jilly up while Maureen flagged down a waitress, calling the harried-looking woman by name.

"Oh, don't worry about your tab, Mo. The boss said it's on the house. See you next Wednesday, like always?"

Stephanie had never seen her aunt blush that hard

before. The older woman mumbled, "Yeah, see you then. Say goodnight to him for me, will you?" And hustled out the door ahead of the others.

"Well, well," Reid observed from close behind Steph's shoulder. "Seems as though the saxophone war has taken a new turn."

Stephanie didn't disagree, nor did she try to hide the fine tremor that rippled through her at the touch of his breath on the back of her neck. Now was not the time for such things.

She straightened her shoulders, tightened her grip on Jilly and stepped back into the night, where the shadows seemed to press closer, held at bay only by the man at her side.

THE WALK from the jazz club to Stephanie's house seemed to take forever, but cabs were scarce and they were in a hurry. Reid would've liked to take his weapon in hand and fan it into every passing alley. He would've liked a helicopter hovering overhead, lighting the narrow cobbled streets and flushing away all the lurking shadows.

He would've liked more backup than two women and a three-year-old kid.

There was the sound of breaking glass from his left, and he shoved Maureen out of the way and braced himself between the women and the alley. There was a high-pitched giggle and a man's voice, slurred with drink.

"Jumpy, Detective?" He flinched when Stephanie touched his hand and the contact seemed to arc straight to the banked blaze in his stomach. He wasn't sure what had him more worked up—her continued proximity or the feeling lodged in his gut that this could all go to hell in an instant.

He nodded. "Yeah. Jumpy."

They continued to walk, and he could see that her energy was flagging. "Here, let me." Though it would cripple him as a protector, he took the child's heavy, sleeping weight and draped it over his shoulder. Steph sighed in relief.

"Thanks. I can't believe how heavy she's getting."

Reid didn't reply as he herded the anxious, tired group up the granite steps to Stephanie's townhouse. She pawed through her bag for the key to the front door.

As he carried the kid up the stairs to the second floor, Reid couldn't help noticing that she smelled of a soft, feminine combination of flowers and chocolate, and her warm, boneless weight felt solid and trusting in his arms. Like She Devil when she napped, all that edgy energy gone completely limp.

Aware that Stephanie was only a step behind him, Reid laid the child on her mother's big bed and stepped back. He didn't look into Stephanie's eyes, fearing the warmth he might see there. The offer of family.

Without a word, he turned and headed for the kitchen.

It took Steph two minutes to tuck Jilly in for the night, five to stomp down the soft emotions that had risen up at the sight of tough guy Reid Peters putting her daughter to bed, and another ten to strangle the irritation his abrupt departure had created.

She would've rather strangled him. Who did he think he was? It wasn't like she'd *asked* him to carry her daughter up to bed. And so what if for a very brief moment her heart had melted at the sight of those big, strong hands cradling Jilly as though she was something precious? Something loved?

So what? She was over it now. Common sense had reasserted itself. He didn't want kids, and he didn't want her. He was doing his job and she was a *victim*. End of story.

She showered and dressed in a pair of black bike shorts, a soft lime-green T-shirt and no bra, thinking, *Eat your heart out, Detective.* Padding down the stairs to the kitchen, she noticed a blinking red light in the living room. "I have one new message," she said to the room at large, and heard a kitchen chair creak in response.

She stabbed the answering machine button as Peters appeared in the doorway.

"This message isn't for you, bitch." She gasped and held her hands over her ears as though blocking out the cold, cruel voice would make it all go away. Why hadn't she thought it would be him? How could she have forgotten the way the dark sibilance could reach through the telephone and grab her by the throat?

Reid cursed and crossed the room to her as the

voice continued. "It's for the cop. Do I have your attention yet? Are you ready to do your job? Well, here it is. You and the lab whore are going to make that evidence disappear." There was a pause and the tape hissed with dead air, then, "If you come anywhere near me, they're all dead. Got it? Because I've already shown you that I know what whores deserve…" The voice faded, then came back stronger. "Maybe I'll even let you decide, cop. The aunt…the child…or the mother? Who goes first?"

Reid cursed again as the tape ended and the machine beeped. Steph could feel his heart beating strong and fast beneath her fingertips when he grabbed her in his arms. She didn't resist when he pulled her close.

But she found no comfort in it, either. She was too afraid.

An hour later, Reid still wanted to punch something. Break something. Kick the wall until his loafer broke through to the cobblestone street outside and kept going. But he knew that wouldn't really solve anything.

So he paced instead.

Sturgeon sat at the kitchen table with Stephanie while the technicians monkeyed with her answering machine the way they were supposed to have done the day before. Maureen leaned weakly against the counter and Mortimer stood beside her looking as though it would take an army to move him. The kid had mercifully slept through all of it.

"So, what happens now?" Stephanie asked, her voice low and flat, just as it had been ever since he'd set her away from him to call Sturgeon and the precinct, in that order.

He'd never, ever in his life felt such a wash of pure, white-hot rage as he had when the voice on the answering machine had threatened Stephanie, her daughter and Maureen in one breath. Reid spun on his heel and paced back across the kitchen, imagining a shadowed face with his fist planted squarely in the center of it.

"The bomb and the phone call don't change anything." Sturgeon answered. "You'll go to the lab with Detective Peters and work the DNA evidence and Maureen and Jilly will stay with Mortimer."

"I want more protection for them than that," Reid snarled. "Put a couple of uniforms on the house and the street."

But Sturgeon shook his head. "Not visibly. We'll have officers in place, but we'll want them to keep a low profile."

"Bait?" Peters's voice cracked, it climbed so high. "You're using them as bait? No way, no how. I want them out of here. Today."

"No," Sturgeon countered. "We're not using civilians as bait, you know better than that. They'll be fully protected, it just won't be obvious. Besides, what else would you have them do, hop a plane to Fiji?"

Reid nodded. "Yes. Fiji. Everyone clears out until all this is over. Great idea."

"I was kidding," Sturgeon mumbled, and Reid scowled.

"Well I'm not. I want them all someplace safe until we've got this guy. He's escalating. You said so yourself. What do you think comes next?" A parade of images flashed through Reid's mind. Red curls in the center of a stained bedspread. A dark-haired girl curled around a rag doll, each more bloody than the other.

"I'm not going anywhere," Stephanie said, and Reid scowled, thinking of handcuffing her and loading her aboard a plane bound for somewhere far away. Someplace safe.

"You want your daughter in danger? Your aunt? How about yourself? Getting you out of here makes the most sense and you know it."

She shook her head, making red curls fly in a cheerful manner that was at odds with their discussion. "I need to stay here, Detective."

"Why? So you can make sure I'm doing my job right?" He cursed. "I'm not your ex-husband," he said. I'm not my father, he thought but didn't say, because some days he wasn't sure. "And I'm not that piece of crap you dated last year. I won't let you down."

"I didn't think you would." Though they both knew she didn't fully trust him.

The anger rose, and he beat it back with a mental fist before he spoke. "Then why won't you go?"

Reid noticed that Sturgeon was following the

exchange with fascination. Well, screw him. Stephanie was leaving whether she liked it or not.

She shrugged, lifted her hands to the sky as if to say *What can I do?* and said, "I have to stay, Reid. With Genie gone, I'm the only one in the lab who's checked out on the DNA database as an analyst. Molly hasn't taken the test yet, and Jared's only qualified as a technician. He can run the experiments, but he can't get into the software. I need to stay here and run the DNA or we might not find him." She glanced at her aunt. "But Maureen and Jilly should leave. I'll work better knowing they're safe."

Maureen spoke up, "Mortimer has a cabin on the New Hampshire border. We could go there for a few days." She colored slightly. "It's…on a lake, not too far from this little town that has a great diner and…well, we could go there."

"Aunt Maureen!" Steph pretended shock, and the ripple of humor relaxed the small group slightly. "Did you *ever* go play bingo on Wednesday nights? And those weekend casino trips with the girls—did you ever even *see* a roulette wheel?"

Maureen's voice was faint when she said, "No, but we have played the occasional hand of strip poker."

"And the battles over the saxophone next door?"

Mortimer answered with a sly grin that had answering color blooming in Maureen's cheeks. "It's not so much the battles as the making up."

Reid knew from talking to Maureen across Steph's hospital bed that the older woman had been widowed young and soon after had inherited her orphaned niece, leaving little time for relationships. Stephanie must have known how hard it had been for her aunt, because from somewhere deep within her, she dredged up a huge smile and a hug for her aunt and Mortimer.

"I'm so happy for both of you. This is wonderful!" Then she sobered. "Go to your cabin and be safe, okay? You can leave first thing in the morning." She swallowed hard. "Take Jilly with you, and if…" She faltered.

"There won't be any 'ifs', Stephanie. We'll see you as soon as this is over. Reid will keep you safe." Maureen patted her niece on the shoulder and fixed Reid with a look that said, *Keep her safe, or else.*

He nodded. He'd keep her safe or die trying.

THAT NIGHT Reid slept in Jilly's bed again. Or rather, he paced through the old house, slinking from window to window and peering out into the crooked nooks of darkness. He learned that the fourth stair from the top creaked loudly if he stepped on the center of it, but not if he stayed to the side. He discovered that the refrigerator hummed to life every thirty-eight minutes or so, and that he wished he had She Devil there for company.

One of the things he liked best about having the cat was that he wasn't alone any more when he got up in the middle of the night to read or lift weights. There was someone who noticed he was awake.

Reid tensed at a downstairs window. Was that

movement? A man waiting for him to let his guard down long enough to take Stephanie and her daughter? He stared at the black on black long enough for colors to begin swimming in front of his eyes before he decided that no, it was nothing. Just his imagination, like the way he imagined that he could feel Stephanie on his skin when he'd barely touched her in hours. Like the way he imagined that he could taste her kiss on his lips, though he'd told her it wouldn't happen again.

Couldn't happen again.

He gripped the windowsill until his knuckles whitened in the hollow light of the moon, then he paced some more. It was crazy, he knew, to keep thinking of a woman he would never have.

He smelled her on the stuffy night air and realized he was standing in the doorway to her room. She was lying sprawled across the covers, and he could see in the splashing moonlight that her forehead was wrinkled. She was frowning in her sleep. He couldn't blame her. She was sending her aunt and daughter away the next day, and entrusting her own safety to a man who was ruled as much by anger as by justice.

He felt his own frown and ordered his face to ease. He should crunch himself up on the kid's bed and try to get a few hours of sleep. Morning would come soon enough. The job would intrude soon enough, reminding him that she was the victim and he stood between her and a voice on the phone that promised dire retribution. Reminded him that he couldn't be distracted when her life was in danger.

But he was unable to turn away from the sight of the little child's hand clutched possessively around the strap of Stephanie's nightgown. After a moment, a burble of sound alerted him that the kid was close to awake. He stepped farther into the room and held a finger to his lips when she looked up at him.

"Shh. Mommy needs her sleep," he whispered, and the child nodded solemnly with those wise old eyes that had already seen too much. She smiled. He backed away. "No way. Last night was a fluke, kid. I'm going back to my room."

She whistled a couple of notes, from that same damn melody she'd been repeating over and over, and stretched her arms toward him. He thought her little lips mouthed a word.

"Aw, heck." He crossed the room in two strides, sat in the protesting rocking chair, and gathered her onto his lap. She was going away the next day. He wouldn't have to see her again, right? And nobody had to know about this. Nobody.

But as her head sagged against his chest and his own eyelids lowered, he thought he saw her lips move again. Thought he heard a whispered word.

"'Tek-tif.''

Because he knew nobody was looking, he touched his lips to her hair. "Yeah Jilly. I'm the detective. I'm going to keep you and your mommy and Auntie Maureen safe. I promise."

But as he slid toward sleep, Reid feared it was his turn to be the liar.

SHE SHOULD BE a better person, Stephanie thought the next morning, than to be jealous of her own daughter. But as she waved Mortimer's car off and suppressed a pang at the sight of Jilly's little fingers pressed against the window in farewell, she couldn't help thinking that she wouldn't mind spending the night draped across Detective Peters's chest like her daughter had. Twice.

Stop it, she told herself sternly. *Don't go there.* Just because he didn't act like the child-hater he claimed to be didn't mean he was any less of a bad choice for a relationship. He worked too hard, slept too little, left the toilet seat up in a house full of women, and he kept such tight control on his temper, she had to wonder what it was like when he lost it.

No, Reid Peters wasn't exactly the man of her dreams.

But then again, Luis had certainly acted dreamy…until the day he'd emptied their joint bank account, the college fund she'd started for their eight-month-old daughter and the cookie jar full of 'fun money' and had taken off for Mexico with the feds on his tail.

That alone had almost been enough to bar her from being cleared to use the national DNA database, but Genie's husband, Nick Wellington, had leaned on a few of his senator father's friends and the way had been cleared. He'd joked it was the biggest use he'd had for his father in years. Steph thought that was too bad. She still missed her dad some days, even though both her parents had been gone a good twenty years, leaving Maureen to raise her alone.

Now it was up to Maureen to protect the grand-child they would never meet. And it was up to Steph to solve the mystery and bring Jilly and Maureen back safely.

She sighed, realizing she'd been staring down an empty cobbled street for several minutes. She turned to Reid. "Sorry. Woolgathering. You ready to go to work?"

He nodded. "Yeah. Let's go get the bastard."

But it wasn't quite that easy, as they learned as soon as they'd translated the DNA results into marker sizes and inputted them to the federal con-victed offenders database.

No match.

"What does that mean?"

Steph bared her teeth. "What does it look like? There's no DNA match in the convicted offenders database. He's not in there. Damn it!" She slapped the desk in frustration as all the hopes she'd pinned on this one experiment shattered into a million pieces.

She glared at the computer. He wasn't in there. Then she glanced at the window, where Chinatown bustled with life thirteen stories down.

He was out there. And he was going to hurt her.

Damn it! She'd been so sure this was the answer.

Reid touched her shoulder and she flinched away. She couldn't stand for him to be nice to her now. She felt as though she was close to falling apart, and that when she did, nothing would put her back to-gether again.

She smiled grimly. Just call her Humpty Dumpty.

Reid withdrew his hand. "Is that the only index you can query?"

"No. There are others. That was just the one that works the best. There are state and local indexes, as well as forensics uploads and missing persons, but they don't come with names and addresses, only the knowledge that the voice matches another unsolved case or a missing person."

Reid sighed. "Okay, you try those databases. I'm going to call Sturgeon and see if we have a plan B." He strode from the computer room and Steph fol-lowed him with her eyes, wondering whether she would ever grow tired of watching him. Wondering whether she would ever see him again once this was over.

Wondering whether this would ever *be* over and if her family would survive it.

On a bitter sigh, she turned back to the computer and got to work.

Reid found her an hour later, still scowling at the screen. It was blinking *No match. No match. No match. No match.*

"I swear to God," Steph muttered, "the next time I see those words on this screen, I'm going to scream bloody murder."

The word *murder* bounced around the empty com-puter room and they both cringed. "Ready for a break?" he asked, noticing the circles beneath her eyes and the defeated slump of her shoulders. He would have touched her then, but she'd shied away from him earlier and he couldn't blame her. If he and Sturgeon had been smarter and luckier, they might have already caught the guy, and Steph could have gone back to her normal life.

But the police, like the lab computer, had come up with nothing. *No match.*

"Break?" She pushed away from the computer and spun her chair irritably. "Yeah, I guess. I'm not getting anywhere here, which makes no sense. Why was he worried about DNA evidence if he's not in the database?"

"Maybe he doesn't understand enough genetics to know you need something to compare it to," Reid suggested.

"Maybe," she agreed, but she didn't sound like she believed it. "But I've got this feeling…"

"Yeah, I know all about those. Come on, let's get some lunch. This will all be here when you get back." Unless another mail bomb was delivered to the computer room, Reid thought without humor. But it was Saturday so the lab floor was deserted, and they'd given strict instructions to the lobby guard that all packages had to be cleared through Sturgeon or himself.

They were as safe as he could make them for the moment, he thought as they walked shoulder to shoulder into Chinatown and left the hospital behind.

"Did Detective Sturgeon have a plan B?"

Reid shook his head as he eyed the thronging pedestrians at the crosswalk. The perp could walk right by them and he'd be none the wiser. Until they had a name or a witness or some new evidence, they had nothing. *No match.* "He's working the Moreplease case as fast as he can, and going back over Wong at the same time. We were really hoping the DNA evidence would point us in the right direction."

"Yeah." She tucked her chin into the collar of her shirt. "Me, too. I just can't get past the feeling that he's in there somewhere, you know?"

"I know. How would he know to worry about the DNA evidence unless he's already been exposed to the concept?" As they passed a doorway that advertised Live Nude Girls! Reid scowled at a low-level dealer and sometime informant who obediently melted back into the shadows. He wasn't in the mood for punks today. The anger was there, churning sluggishly and waiting for him to let his control slip. Or maybe it was the sexual energy he felt whenever Stephanie was nearby. He wasn't sure he could tell the difference between the two any more. Both were hot. Both threatened to escape his control.

And both overwhelmed him.

"Maybe his lawyer explained it to him the last time he went through the system." Stephanie paused outside the restaurant she'd chosen. "But if that's the case, how come he's not popping up on any of the searches?"

Reid shrugged and scanned the eddying crowd again. His back itched, damn it. The perp was out there. Somewhere. "I don't know." He held the door open and practically shoved her through, cursing the hot wave that raced up his arm at the contact. He had it bad. But knowing it and doing something about it were two different things. He merely growled, ''Let's eat.''

There was a long wait, so they grabbed takeout instead and wrangled over the choices like a couple who had nothing better to do than debate crab Rangoons versus spring rolls. But through it all there were two layers of tension—the danger and the desire.

Reid was doing his best to deal with the one and didn't have a clue how to stamp out the other.

When they hit the street again, greasy brown bags in hand, he took Steph's arm to hurry her down a narrow alley to the next cross street.

''What's wrong?''

''Nothing. Everything.'' The heat sang up his arm while the spot on his back burned. ''I have a—''

Feeling, he'd meant to say. But the deafening rat-tat-tat of automatic gunfire drowned him out and the itchy spot between his shoulder blades sang like a wound. This was it. The perp had come for her, and to hell with anyone else who got in the way.

Stephanie screamed and covered her ears. Reid yelled, *''No!''* and felt the anger blaze high. He pushed her into a shallow doorway off the alley and yanked his weapon clear. Wanting, needing to see the man who had done all this.

Wanting to kill him.

The hail of noise intensified and Reid heard

screaming out in the cross street beyond. He tensed, wanting to go help but needing to stay with Stephanie. To protect her.

The voice on the phone was coming for her.

Then the gunfire slackened and Reid realized it sounded *wrong* somehow. Like a soundtrack rather the real thing. The noise halted. The screams went on.

Then they were joined by the sound of clapping and hooting.

Cheers. Whistles.

And a last few sharp bangs.

"Reid?" He felt her hand on his shoulder and the warmth of her body against his back. "It's okay. It's just firecrackers. Chinese firecrackers." Her breath feathered against the short hairs at his neck and the lust roared up to meet the anger that spiked at the knowledge that he'd overreacted. Badly.

In the heat of the moment, he had pushed her up against a door and pressed against her so his body would act as a shield. Now, he could feel the press of her breasts against his back and the curve of her groin against his rear. Standing on the single shallow step, she was perfectly aligned with his body.

The pressure excited him.

It undid him.

"Reid?"

He spun and pressed against her, trapping her against the door and leaving her powerless but not caring a bit. He saw the surprise in her blue-green eyes, and the quick flare of temper that matched his own.

He didn't give her a chance to give. He took.

His lips crushed down on hers as their lunch fell to the ground and the anger rose high. Anger at the man who wanted to hurt her. Anger at the situation that made her part of his job and threatened her life. Anger at himself for not being able to stay away. Anger at her for making him feel things he didn't want to feel.

And over it all, the tangling, taunting heat that he called lust because he didn't know a better word.

The flames soared higher, and he realized that far from plundering, he was being met heat for heat, and that her quick, clever hands had worked their way inside his shirt where they teased and took without mercy.

He fastened his mouth on her throat and her head tipped back. She moaned when he took possession of her breast and he felt the beast within him roar with a primitive, undeniable hunger. He was hard and aching where he pressed against her, frustrated and excited at the same time by the layers of cloth that separated them.

He kissed her mouth again, almost dying from the feel of it when she sucked his tongue deep and hooked one leg high around his waist so he could press home more fully. He caught her thigh and felt the heat through her thin linen slacks. Felt her shiver when he scraped his fingernails along the inner seam and thought he might howl with the power and the want of it all.

Catching her other leg, he boosted her up so he was pressing her fully against the filthy alley doorway, thrusting into her with his tongue and his throbbing, confined length until they were both panting into each other's mouths and there was no sight, no sound. Only feeling.

The feeling of the woman against him. His woman.

And the knowledge, like the firecrackers that rattled again in the street beyond like gunfire, yanked him back to the reality of who she was. Who he was. Where they were.

Reid froze.

He was dry-humping his protectee in a Chinatown alley.

Oh, hell.

This was about as unprofessional as it got. And stupid. He glanced around the alley. And dangerous. Six big guys could have come up behind him and he wouldn't have known.

Wouldn't have cared.

He unwrapped her legs from his waist and stepped away, shoved his hands in his pockets so she wouldn't see how badly they shook, and took a breath.

"Don't you dare," she hissed. Her jade eyes snapped with temper and her fine-boned hands were clenched at her sides.

Reid wondered whether Botticelli had ever painted *Venus on a Rampage*. "I—"

"*No!*" she cut him off again. "You don't get to walk this time, Peters. You don't just get to kiss me when you feel like it and turn away when it gets messy." She took a step toward him, and damned if he didn't find himself backing away.

She poked a finger in his chest and he noticed his shirt was undone except where the shoulder holster had cinched it shut. He felt the scrape of her nail across his skin and fought not to shudder. Fought not to reach for her.

"I didn't mean to—"

"Not this time, buster." Oddly, her temper soothed his own, and he fought an urge to grin when she poked him in the chest again. "You don't get to walk away this time. It's my turn." She brushed past him and called over her shoulder, "Don't kiss me again until you mean it, Peters. And I'll thank you to remember that I'm nobody's victim."

This time, when she walked toward the roaring noise of leftover firecrackers from the Chinese New Year, Reid didn't try to stop her. He followed, thinking to himself that he'd make damned sure she was nobody's victim.

But he feared he would become hers.

Chapter Nine

Steph marched back to the lab and left Reid to follow with the crumpled bags of Chinese food that had more or less survived her brush with danger and stupidity in the alley. Danger from what had turned out to be firecrackers. Stupidity for letting him kiss her again. For kissing him back.

They didn't speak until they were alone in the elevator, riding back up to thirteen.

"I don't think you're a victim." He stared at the blinking floor lights as he said it. "I never have."

"Then why say it?" It had hurt more than it probably should have, because part of Steph saw herself that way. As Luis's victim. Roger's. Well, no more. She refused to cry and hide. She was going to fight if it kill…well, she was going to fight.

"I was reminding myself that you're off limits. You're under my protection as an officer. That makes you my job." They reached thirteen and he waited in the lobby while she keyed in the code to unlock the security door.

She stomped past him, still churned up by his

kisses, still ticked off by how easy he found it to turn her away. "You've got a strange way of keeping me off limits, Peters. Do me a favor and don't touch me again, okay? I'm not looking for a quickie in a Chinatown alley." Though she would have settled for it fifteen minutes ago and the future be damned. "And I'm not making another mistake with the wrong guy. It'll be Jilly and me for a while. If I let a guy into that, he has to be there for the long haul and he has to want to be a father to Jilly."

They entered the computer room and she felt the edgy tension rise in him as he brushed past her to stand before the computer she'd been working on. Without looking at her, he said, "I'm not that guy, Steph."

Though it had been obvious all along, it still hurt to hear. She nodded and he glanced over. Their eyes locked and held.

"No match?" he asked quietly.

She nodded again. "No match." She sighed and sat down at the computer, acutely aware of his nearness as she logged back on. She could taste him in her mouth and feel the lingering dampness between her legs where she'd been ready for him to take her there, standing up in a filthy alley in the back of beyond.

It would have been wonderful, she knew. And it would have been terrible, because after that there would be no going back. No pretending they weren't barreling down the path to self-destruction and heartache.

She sighed again as *No match* flashed on the screen once again. It was time to get back to work. She cracked her knuckles and poised her fingers above the keyboard. Then she began to run searches as she thought out loud.

"We think he thinks his DNA is on file somewhere, which means he was arrested for a crime that would call for a DNA sample to be taken." She cross-checked the markers from the Makepeace sample against an obscure database run by an upstate New York college. No match.

"That's not much help," Reid mused. As he paced the confines of the small room, he reminded Steph of a caged animal. Feral and primitive. All long, hard muscles and sleek skin. *Stop it,* she told herself fiercely and tried to pay attention to what he was saying. "...takes DNA samples for most felonies at this point, so he could've been arrested for most anything."

The sound of the lobby buzzer interrupted them. Steph reached for the Admit button beside the computer-room door, but Reid held up a hand. "I'll get it."

He drew his gun and went to answer the door. Steph shuddered at the reminder that locks or no, police protection or no, she was still in grave danger. She thought of Jilly and was glad she and Maureen were far away with Mortimer to protect them.

She thought of Reid and shivered again, knowing that it was foolish to want him, and wanting him just the same.

REID RETURNED to the computer room with Sturgeon right behind him. He took one look at Stephanie sitting at the computer in her oversized white lab coat and felt his temperature spike.

He didn't want a kid or a family, but he wanted *her*.

"Any ideas?" Sturgeon asked.

Reid shook his head, reminding himself to think of the job. The job, not the woman. "I think the DNA is played out for now." He saw Steph's shoulders slump and scowled. "We'll have to hit the pavement and turn over a few rocks in Chinatown. There's enough bad blood in the neighborhood that somebody will turn if we lean hard enough."

It sounded good in theory, but the detectives both knew the process could take weeks or months. And they both agreed that the escalating pattern of violence suggested that Stephanie and her family had mere days before the perp tried something else. What had begun as a simple blackmail had evolved into an obsession. The DNA evidence was an excuse for him now, nothing more.

The man on the phone simply wanted to hurt Stephanie and her daughter. Kill them for the joy of it. The sport. They had become *his*.

Reid consciously relaxed his fingers, which ached from being balled into tense fists.

He heard her whisper, "Bad blood."

"What?" Sturgeon perked up. Reid noticed that Steph's shoulders had straightened and a spark of battle had entered her eyes.

"Bad blood," she repeated. "You said something about bad blood, right?"

Reid nodded. "Most of the locals are related somehow, and those that aren't are feuding with each other at any given moment."

She grinned suddenly. "I have an idea. Give me five minutes."

The detectives crowded closer as she pulled up a search engine and changed several boxes from 1.0 to 0.5. She exited the code and got back to a main screen. "Right now, we're looking for a name, right? Or at least a direction."

"Right," Reid said, getting an inkling of what she had in mind. He felt the first glimmer of a tingle in his chest. It was the opposite of the itch on his back. The tingle meant things were starting to go right.

Maybe.

Fingers flying, she entered the data from the rape kits. "So I've adjusted the search parameters to give us any names that match by fifty percent or better, rather than the hundred percent we usually search by."

"What will that do?" Sturgeon bit down on a fresh candy and tucked the crinkling wrapper into his pocket.

"Well," she replied as she hit Enter and sat back while the computer whirred and said Processing. "If everyone's related to everyone around here, maybe family members of his have been uploaded into the local database for having committed crimes of their own."

Reid asked, "Is that legal?" at the same time Sturgeon asked, "Why just the local database?"

Steph grimaced. "Legally, it's borderline. Not all of this type of work has been reliably legislated yet, and that's why we're just searching the local database. First off, if he's related, chances are he's local. And second," The computer began uploading a new screen and all three of them leaned forward in anticipation, "The local database is administered through you guys. I'm not brave enough to mess with a federal search engine."

The graphics loaded slowly. As they waited, Reid asked, "Couldn't you lose your certification if anyone found out?"

She slid her eyes toward him and he felt the punch low in his gut. "Do you think I give a rat's ass about that when Maureen's and Jilly's lives are at stake?"

Reid was saved from answering when three lines popped onto the screen.

Lucas Reynolds—.58 match.
Sinclair Bott—.53 match.
Simon Bott—.53 match.

And all of a sudden, they had names.

Reid felt the anger flare and swore in that moment to personally track down each one of them and hurt them for daring to go after Stephanie.

Daring to go after his woman.

STEPH YELLED after his retreating back, "Where are you going?"

"Get back here," Sturgeon barked. "Those names aren't the guy, remember?"

She was surprised. Of the two of them, Reid had always been more interested in the genetics being done at the lab. She would've expected him to grasp the concept of her search before Sturgeon did, but it had been Reid running out the door with a murderous set to his jaw and a sharp gold gleam of anger in his eyes.

She'd never thought of Detective Peters as impulsive.

But perhaps *Reid* was. And perhaps his feelings for her went deeper than she thought. Deeper than he thought—or would admit.

"Yeah, right. Sorry." He retook his seat, pulling it close enough to the computer that Stephanie could feel his heat at her back, feel the anger spiked with frustration. Or was that her frustration? "Relatives. I forgot. So all three of these guys are related to our perp?"

Steph shifted screens and tapped an inquiry. "Not necessarily. We're playing a game of averages. On average, parents, children and siblings share fifty percent of their DNA. But they can also randomly share stretches of DNA with unrelated people. Since we're only looking at data from thirteen markers, it's possible that our bad guy shares half of them with an unrelated person just by chance."

The computer spat out three sheets of paper as Reid asked, "So how can we tell which is which? Guess?"

Steph told herself to ignore his tone. She felt it

too—the itchy, twitchy restlessness that said they were getting closer to the answer. The shifting heat that said they were getting closer to each other when they should have been moving apart.

It was too much. And too little.

"No," she replied. "No guessing. Now we back it down a level and look at the markers themselves. If our bad guy is the parent or child of one—or more of these guys," she said, thinking of the two men on the list with identical surnames, "they will share one copy of each of the thirteen markers, right?"

Sturgeon cocked an eyebrow. "And if they're brothers?"

"Then we have to work the averages," Steph admitted. She pulled the sheets from the printer tray and compared them to the DNA samples they'd been flogging all morning. She whistled.

"Got something?" Reid leaned over her shoulder and she felt his breath on a previously undiscovered sensitive spot behind her ear. She trembled slightly, and heard his breath catch. Felt the temperature in the computer room skyrocket.

And focused harder on the printouts. "Yes, I've got something." She set aside the printout labeled Reynolds and placed the other two side by side.

Sinclair and Simon Bott's markers matched exactly. They were a hundred percent identical. And when she placed the DNA profiles from the rape kits beside the Botts' printouts, it was obvious that they shared one copy of each marker.

"I thought you said that a hundred-percent DNA match only happened if it was the same person," Reid challenged.

Steph shook her head. "There's one case where that's not true. Identical twins." She tapped Simon and Sinclair's printouts. "These two are identical twins, and one of them is either the father or the son of the voice on the phone."

They got it. Sturgeon was already on the phone.

Reid leaned forward and kissed her on the cheek. "You're amazing." Then he stood and reached for his own phone. "Let's get to work."

TWENTY MINUTES LATER, Reid cursed and slapped the phone shut. He shook his head. "Sinclair's kids have juvenile records, but we're going to have to petition for access. I don't think I explained the fifty percent thing very well." He paced the little room, scratching the middle of his back with a pencil. "We don't have that much time."

And that, more than anything, told Steph that he felt it, too. They were running out of time. Something bad was going to happen.

She had a sudden urge to call Mortimer's cabin yet again and make sure Maureen and Jilly were safe. Instead, she leaned forward to readjust the search parameters for the local database and bump them back up to a hundred percent match. And paused.

Bott.

Reid's head came up, and she wondered whether she had made a noise. Or perhaps he was as attuned to her as she was to him. Scary thought. "Find something else?"

"No. Not exactly." She exited the local database and brought up the lab's main menu.

"Well, what exactly?" Sturgeon asked, closing his own phone.

She was aware of the men crowding back around her, wondered if they expected a miracle. Well, she just might be able to deliver. "When we first started subcontracting for you, I ran a set of samples on a man named Bott." She felt a frisson of excitement as she found the proper file.

"Sinclair Bott's samples might have come through here," Sturgeon remarked. "He's upstate for aggravated assault."

Steph shook her head. "Not Sinclair. Not Simon either. Aha!" She found the gel number listed in the film database. The results weren't computerized because there had been no reason to scan them. DNA wasn't uploaded if the defendant was found not guilty. "Derek Bott. Charged with date rape."

Sturgeon nodded. "Right. According to Chinatown station records, Simon Bott's been out of circulation for six years and doesn't have any kids. Sinclair has five boys, one of which—Derek—beat a rape count earlier this year when he claimed to have had consensual sex with the girl earlier in the evening and had an alibi for the time of the attack. The girl backed out at the last minute and the case was dropped."

The detectives followed Steph out of the computer

room and into the hall outside Genie Watson's office, where the majority of the archived films were stored in long gray filing cabinets. The smell of charred plastic and cleaning solution was more pronounced out here, and Steph thought briefly of the scorched wreck that used to be her desk. Thought of her daughter and aunt. She glanced at the retrieval number and slid open the appropriate drawer.

"So if you've run Derek Bott's DNA before, why didn't his name come up on any of the searches?" Reid asked.

She pulled the film out and held it up to the light, as though she might be able to tell right then and there if he was the one. Then she snorted at the fancy. They were just black bars on a gray piece of film.

But if they matched the other films back at the desk she'd appropriated from Jared...

"He wasn't convicted," Sturgeon pointed out. Steph nodded.

"Exactly. We're lucky the experiment was run here and that I remembered the name."

"In other words," Reid followed the information to its logical conclusion as they marched through to the Wellington lab. "Our access to this DNA data is illegal, unethical and completely inadmissible in court."

Steph slapped the films on the light box. "Yeah. Got a problem with that?"

He shoved his hands in his pockets and scowled.

"No," he said. "No problem at all until it's time for a warrant or a conviction."

"Just get him away from me and my family," she said as she flicked on the fluorescent bulb of the light box. "That's all I care about."

Black bars sprang to life against transparent gray film and Reid cursed bitterly. Triumphantly.

The name *Derek Bott* was written across the top of the new film in Genie's familiar MD scrawl, but it could just as well have read *Wong,* or *Moreplease.*

Because the markers were identical.

"Let's go get him," Reid said.

Sturgeon grinned fiercely. "Right behind you."

Reid turned to her and she saw his eyes blaze with determination. "Engage the night locks behind us and wait here, okay? I'll call when there's news and I'll put a uniform in the lobby." Steph nodded numbly.

Hope that this would end it all warred with fear that Reid might be hurt and lodged like a ball in her throat. She felt tears press, but willed them back. Felt words hover but couldn't voice them. Wanted to kiss him good luck but didn't have the nerve.

Wanted to kiss him goodbye but didn't have the heart.

So she locked the door behind the detectives and sat down at Jared's desk to wait. When the phone rang, she let the machine pick it up.

The heavy breathing lasted a long time before he giggled and hung up.

Stephanie put her face in her hands and wept.

Chapter Ten

Normally, Reid didn't mind waiting for all the pieces to be in place. Right now, it was driving him insane. He wanted this done. Now.

"If this was the Old West, we could just go in, shoot the place up and be done with it," he snarled as he shifted position in Sturgeon's wife's minivan for the fifth time in as many minutes. "Instead we're stuck here waiting."

"Look, do you need to go to the bathroom or something?" Sturgeon growled in his best if-I-have-to-stop-this-car-you'll-be-sorry voice. "Because either go take a walk and leave me in peace or sit down, shut up and stop squirming. We have zero probable cause that we can go on record with, so we have to wait for the go-ahead."

Which meant hoping the others could rustle up a reason to bring Bott in for questioning that had nothing to do with his father's DNA. Until then, they were stuck making sure Bott stayed away from Stephanie and her family.

Sighing, Sturgeon returned to watching the once

lovely, now slightly seedy place across the street from them. The faded green house squatted on a bare patch of ground between two hulking brick apartment buildings. At the border between Chinatown and the Theater District, a few of these neighborhoods persisted in spite of the high-crime, low-income flavor.

Or perhaps because of it.

"I'm not squirming," said Reid, and defiantly uncrossed his legs and crossed them again. "I think I'm getting hives from being in the mommymobile. If we had to wait, why couldn't we at least have used my car?"

He knew the complaint sounded suspiciously like a whine. Perhaps it was a function of the minivan. Or perhaps it was something else.

Something itchy and hot with an unfamiliar sensation running through it that didn't feel quite like anger. Didn't feel quite like lust. But certainly felt like something complicated and not at all welcome in Reid's life.

"Because this blends into the area better," Sturgeon replied. He was right. The few cars parked along the narrow road were an odd blend of SUVs and junkers. "And if Bott's been watching Stephanie's place, he probably knows your car."

Reid couldn't argue with that. He glanced at his watch. Still five-fifteen. "There's a good chance that District Attorney Hedlund has gone home for the night without getting our warrant."

"Patience," Sturgeon cautioned. "This is tricky.

We had no legal right to access Sinclair Bott's DNA, and since Derek was cleared of the date-rape charge, his data should've been destroyed. Richard is going to have to do some tap dancing to even get us the warrant. Have faith.''

"Sorry," Reid muttered. "I'm fresh out of that." He shifted on the cushy seat and wrinkled his nose at the smell of graham crackers and apple juice. "Give me a mint, will you?"

Sturgeon just slid him a look and passed one over. "Relax. Stephanie'll be okay."

"Did I say I was worried about her?" Reid snapped back. "Of course she'll be fine. Her and the kid both." He would see to it if it killed him. Then he'd leave her to find the man of her dreams—the one who'd be a father to the kid and the lover Steph wanted.

Reid relaxed the fist he'd made at the thought of Stephanie in another man's bed. At the thought of the kid sleeping in another man's lap.

He hated the guy already.

"The kid's name is Jilly."

"You think I don't know that?" Reid shot back. "Of course I know that. I just…" He trailed off. He just what? He just didn't want to use her name because that made her more real? Made her more vulnerable to the awful things human beings did to each other?

Or because the child was the first, last and best reason he couldn't chase after Stephanie? Because no kid deserved a cop for a father.

Sturgeon's cell phone rang. "Sturgeon." Reid's partner paused to listen, then nodded into the phone. "Got it. Thanks for trying."

Reid groaned when Sturgeon hung up. "D.A. Hedlund couldn't get the search warrant, could he?"

"No. We're going to have to bring Derek in for questioning and hope he gives us enough to hold him on." Sturgeon shrugged. "Couldn't really expect anything more, honestly."

But deep down, Reid had hoped for more. He'd hoped for a warrant that would allow him to toss Bott's mangy house, break a few dishes, maybe even slash a cushion or two before they dragged his scrawny ass down to Chinatown for questioning. Because when Bott messed with Stephanie and her family, he messed with Reid Peters. It was as simple as that.

And as complicated.

Sturgeon spoke into the radio, nodded at the response, and glanced over. "He's still in there. Jenks and Spiro have the back door. We'll knock on the front and ask him to come along all friendly and answer a few questions."

Reid checked his weapon, leaving his suit coat unbuttoned for easy access. "Yeah, and if we're lucky he'll resist arrest and yell 'hide the dope' so we'll have probable cause to search that dump."

Sturgeon snorted. "Yeah, and you really hate kids as much as you pretend, too."

"What's that supposed to mean?" But Sturgeon was gone, easing out of the mommymobile and sauntering across the street as though oblivious to the sudden quiet and the subtle twitch of curtain here and there.

"Hey, wait up!" Reid jogged to his partner's side just as Sturgeon knocked on the flimsy screen door, dislodging a shower of paint chips from the flaky siding.

"Derek Bott? Bott, are you in there?" Sturgeon called, and was answered by a series of scuffling noises. "Bott? Come out, or we're coming in."

Not waiting for a reply, Reid yanked the screen door open—almost ripping it off the one flimsy hinge that still supported it—and yelled, "Come on out, Derek. We just want to ask you a few questions. All nice and friendly, okay?"

He heard Sturgeon mutter, "Yeah, that sounded friendly, all right," as he stomped into the house, trusting his partner to back him up. The scuffling at the back of the house suddenly intensified to a series of thumps, and the radio at Sturgeon's hip spat to life.

"He's going out the back!" Reid accelerated down the hall, barely registering the young woman huddled on the living-room sofa with a pair of identical little boys clutched to her breast. The radio squealed again and Sturgeon cursed.

"He got past Jenks. I'll get the car and meet you."

Reid tossed an affirmative over his shoulder, took one look at the high, narrow bathroom window that was open just far enough to let Bott's skinny ass through, and kicked his way out the back door.

"Which way?" he yelled to Spiro, who was unsuccessfully trying to crank his squad car over. The youngster was notorious for his ability to kill cars by looking at them. It was an unfortunate gift.

"That way," the kid yelled, pointing. "Jenks is on him."

Reid sprinted, not wasting his breath on his opinion of Jenks's ability in a foot pursuit.

He passed the laboring donut poster boy in a matter of a half minute, and cut through an alley at Jenks's breathless gesture. He didn't see Bott, but Sturgeon's white minivan was waiting at the end of the alley.

"Anything?" Reid asked as he swung into the vehicle.

Sturgeon accelerated away, laying rubber and causing an assortment of squeaky toys to slosh from one side of the back seat to the other. "Spiro just radioed that he cut over toward the open market. He makes it there, we won't find him."

The minivan slithered through a sharp left, and the soda Reid had left in the dashboard cup holder fell, splashing Sturgeon's pants on the way down.

"Damn it. Jen's going to kill me for messing up her car."

Reid ignored Sturgeon and pointed. "There he is. Get closer." He yanked his weapon free and hit the button to lower the passenger-side window. It slid down halfway, then stopped. "What the hell?"

Sturgeon sent the minivan hurtling toward Bott, who was running for all he was worth, straight down a road that provided little cover. Unfortunately, it ended at the Chinatown open market, which was noisy, crowded and a perfect place to hide.

Bott couldn't be allowed to reach the market.

"Kidproof window," Sturgeon explained as he slalomed the minivan between a pair of taxis. "Don't even think about it. Jen would kill me for sure."

Reid lowered the gun he'd planned to use to smash the window out with. "You're kidding."

"I never kid about my wife. I'll get ahead of him and slow down."

Reid rolled his eyes but didn't argue. Sturgeon hit the gas—and swung toward the curb just as Bott swerved toward an alley.

Reid shoved open the passenger door and bounced it off a light post. He heard the scrape of white paint and buckling metal as he jumped out, took two running steps and launched himself at Derek Bott.

He wasn't sure who howled louder, Sturgeon or Bott.

WHEN THE CALL finally came, Steph could barely bring herself to answer it. She stared at the lab phone for a long moment, hoping it was Reid.

Because if it was that cold, cruel voice again, it meant that she was still in danger, and something had happened to her protector.

On the fourth ring, she snatched the handset from its cradle, not willing to wait for the answering machine to click on again and record the breathing and the laughter. "Hello?"

"Miss Alberts? Detective Sturgeon here."

Relief was quick as fear, she found, and as powerful. "Yes, this is Stephanie. Did you get him?"

The detective's voice sounded strangely glum when he replied, "Yes, we did. There was a chase, but Detective Peters apprehended Bott."

"Is everyone okay?" When Sturgeon didn't answer right away, she felt her heartbeat accelerate and pressed, "Is Reid hurt?"

"No, he's fine. A little bruised and banged, but nothing major. My wife's car looks worse than he does."

Steph didn't bother to wonder at the comparison. She was too busy being relieved that Reid was okay and Bott was in custody. "Then it's over? I can call Mortimer and have Aunt Maureen and Jilly come home?"

"Sure," came Sturgeon's easy agreement. "His resisting arrest gave us enough leverage to search Bott's place and request his phone records. Didn't find much in the search, but two calls were made to your house from his number. That should be enough to hold him."

"Thank God." Steph sank down at her lab bench and pressed her forehead to the cool, sterile surface. "It's over."

"Yes, Miss Alberts. Time to get back to your life. We'll be in touch."

Steph heard a familiar voice in the background. "Is that Detective Peters? I'd like to thank him."

There was an awkward pause, then Sturgeon's

voice. "No, ma'am. That was someone else. Like I said, we'll be in touch." And the line went dead.

Stephanie stared at the handset for a long moment before replacing it on the cradle.

She shut down the lights for the night, waved at the watchman, noticed that the uniform guarding the lobby was gone, and let herself through the revolving front door for the walk home.

Alone.

"CARE TO TELL ME why I just lied to her?" Sturgeon shook his head in disappointment. "How many times do I have to tell you that you need a life? That the job gets easier when you have someone waiting for you at home besides a cranky stray cat and a bunch of dead-looking fake plants?"

"Let it lie, Sturgeon." Reid rubbed at his temples, trying to wish the pounding pain away. The pavement had been harder than usual when he'd hit, and Bott's bony knee had almost poked his eyeball through to the back of his skull. All in all, he wasn't up to deflecting Sturgeon's 'why every cop needs a wife' speech.

Particularly when he could still picture those two little boys, huddled against their mother on the couch, watching with wide eyes as big men broke into their house and chased their father down like a dog.

Who was he to bring scenes like that home at the end of the day? He was the job. There wasn't anything left of him besides it. The anger throbbed dully and the tingle in his chest had soured to an ache.

"At least go see her," Sturgeon persisted. "Maureen and Jilly are on their way home and Bott's lawyered up, so we won't be getting much from him until his man arrives tomorrow. Tell her it's all over, if nothing else."

Reid scowled. "I'm not fit company for anyone right now, Sturgeon. I'm going home. To *my* home, and I'm going to take ten or twelve aspirin and sleep through until morning. I'll see you tomorrow."

Sturgeon didn't try to stop him as Reid stomped out of Chinatown station, but he was pretty sure he heard the older man call, "Tell her I said hello, will you?"

Reid called back over his shoulder, "And tell Jen I said hi after you explain the dent in the mommy-mobile, okay?"

Sturgeon cursed explosively and Reid felt a whole world better.

He wouldn't be the only one sleeping alone that night.

IT WAS SURPRISING how much everything changed with the knowledge that Derek Bott was in custody, Steph thought. Mortimer had brought Maureen and Jilly home soon after dark, and when Jilly had cried, "Mama!" Steph had burst into tears and held her daughter tight.

At least *something* good had come of this.

They'd had an early supper and Maureen had gone

to the club with Mortimer with a brilliant smile on her face and an unfamiliar spring in her step. Steph had chatted to her daughter, who was speaking some as well as whistling, and had put her to bed with the new teddy bear Maureen had bought in New Hampshire.

Then Steph had stood in the doorway for a few minutes, watching her daughter sleep.

She prowled the downstairs, making sure the new locks were secure, even though Bott was in custody.

She changed into her lab coat robe, made hot chocolate, drank half and left the rest.

When she heard the knock at the front door, she knew instantly that it was Reid, and she was more relieved that the wait was over than surprised he had come. She'd wanted this, wanted him like she'd wanted nothing else in her life except a healthy baby girl.

And she was ready to fight for him.

She opened the door without a word and held it aside so he could come in, but he stood on the front steps as though he was nailed there. A muscle at the side of his jaw pulsed, and the light from her front hall glanced off the cardboard box at his feet.

"Moving in?" she joked, though her heart was pounding, her stomach starting to sink. He had come, but he didn't look happy about it.

He was wearing the same outfit he'd had on when she'd called him to find Jilly—God, was it only three days ago? The cutoff sweatshirt still clung in all the right places and the jeans still hugged his body like a lover, but the man inside them was different. Distant. Remote.

He stuffed his hands in his pockets and she realized with a start it was the first time in days she'd seen him without his shoulder holster. It made her think that the danger must truly be past.

So where did that leave them?

"I want to ask a favor of you," he said, still not crossing the threshold. He nodded down at the box, which was moving slightly as though being rocked from within. "I'd like you to take She Devil and the kittens. I thought...I thought Jilly might like them."

It was the first time he'd said her daughter's name. Steph felt her lips curve upward even as her heart raced. "Of course they can stay here for a while."

He shook his head. "I want you to keep them. I...I don't have the room for them."

When she understood, the smile drained away. He'd made his decision. He didn't have room for them in his life. He didn't want the ties. Didn't want any of it, not family, not pets. Not love.

Not her.

He'd never claimed any different, but still, the disappointment pierced deep and drew blood. Steph could feel it throbbing beneath the surface, tangling with a hurt so pure it sang a clear, sweet note in her head.

"You came to say goodbye." It wasn't a question.

He nodded tightly. "It's for the best, Steph. Bott is in jail. You're safe. Jilly and Maureen are home.

It's over.'' The few feet between them stretched for miles.

"Why?"

He didn't pretend to misunderstand. His face shut down, though his hands were fisted at his sides. "It wouldn't work, Steph. You know it as well as I."

The knife pierced deeper and she drew a breath and willed the tears back. "I'm not your job any more, Reid. You don't need to protect me from Bott any more."

The muscle at his jaw worked once. Twice. "I'm not talking about Bott and you know it." He stared down at his fisted hand. "I don't do the family thing, okay? I'm sorry. It's just not me."

She wasn't giving up that easily. She stepped closer and watched his eyes glint gold as the hem of the old soft lab coat brushed against his leg. "I don't believe you."

His eyes narrowed. "Unlike some of us, I don't lie."

"Low blow, Peters. Unlike some of us, I don't put myself ahead of my family." She blew out a breath. "That was uncalled for. I'm sorry. I just don't understand. Do you hate children that much?" It didn't make any sense. He'd fallen asleep rocking Jilly.

"I don't hate kids."

"Then what? Are you gay? Already married?"

"No and no," but she'd gotten a ghost of a grin out of him. It soon faded. "I'm a cop."

He said it as though it was a bad thing, as though it should explain everything and his shoulders sagged beneath the weight of it. He was exhausted, Steph realized. He'd been up the past two nights watching over her and Jilly.

Protecting them.

She picked up the cardboard box. "Come inside."

Mutely, he followed her, as though he was too tired to do anything else. When she'd settled the kitties in Jilly's room—she'd be thrilled when she woke up—Steph handed Reid a mug of hot chocolate and sat beside him on the cushy sofa.

"Why can't a cop have a family? Sturgeon seems to manage just fine."

Reid snorted and sagged back against the arm of the couch, as far away from her as he could get and still be on the same piece of furniture. "Sturgeon's a fluke. My father was more the norm. A great cop and a failure as a human being."

Steph thought of the old cigarette burns on his shoulder and winced.

He stared into his cup of hot chocolate. "My mother tried to please him, but it never worked. Most nights he'd come home from work, put away his badge and his gun, and start yelling. Sometimes hitting. When I was little, I'd run upstairs and hide. When I got older, I didn't."

Steph made a wordless sound of distress and reached out to him, placing a hand on his bare forearm that he seemed not to notice.

He glanced sideways at her. "Don't you get it? I'm like he was. When I scared you and Jilly in the kitchen the other day? That could have been my old man in your kitchen. The volume was the same. The anger was the same.''

''*You're* not the same,'' Steph said emphatically, shaking his arm a little. She felt him slipping away from her and could have wept for the pain she saw in the back of his eyes. For the little boy he'd been. ''You were angry with me because I'd lied to you and withheld evidence. You don't think anger is justified there?'' His mouth twisted slightly, encouraging her. ''You're not your father, Reid. And I'm not your mother.''

''I know that. But you're Jilly's mother, and that's a part of you that I can't ignore.''

''I wouldn't want you to. We're a package deal. But I still don't see the problem. I trust you not to hurt her and I trust you not to hurt me.''

He sprang up off the couch and strode across the room and back, scrubbing his hands through his hair. ''Don't you get it? *I* don't trust me, okay? I don't trust the job.'' He stopped in front of her and stared down, exhaustion battling with desperation in his eyes. ''Have you ever seen a dead child, Stephanie? I have. I've seen children killed for no more reason than because they were in the wrong place at the wrong time, or because they were born to the wrong parents. Is that the world you want your daughter to grow up in?''

Steph stood and glared. ''That *is* the world my daughter lives in, Peters, and it's because of men like you and Sturgeon that she'll live long enough to grow up in it. Have I seen a child killed? No, I haven't. But I've seen one born and I'll never forget it. Don't you want that for yourself? Wouldn't knowing that you have someone to come home to make it easier to get through some of the toughest days?''

''You don't understand.'' He seemed almost desperate now, pacing and fisting his hands as though he wanted to fight an enemy he couldn't even name.

She shook her head. ''You're right. I don't understand.'' She stood in his way until he stopped pacing and faced her. ''I understand that with my history I should be the last person to trust my instincts. I know there's no reason why I should want to be with you when you say you have nothing to offer.'' She spread her hands. ''But I'm willing to take that chance. Are you?''

She thought he might walk then and there. Thought he might take her in his arms and kiss the fears away. Thought he might curse and rage again, while being careful never to hurt or scare her.

But she didn't expect him to sink to the sofa and cradle his head in his hands.

''I'm sorry. I can't do this now. I'm so goddamn tired,'' he said. ''So tired.''

And though it wasn't an answer at all, it was an answer of sorts as the strongest man she'd ever known let her see him vulnerable. Nothing was decided between them, but Steph couldn't fight the surge of unexpected tenderness. Didn't try to.

She reached a hand down to him. ''Come upstairs then.''

He stood and looked down at her for an endless

moment, the gold of his eyes mirroring her own desire and confusion. Then he kissed her, gently, and it was all the answer she needed.

After that furious, grappling moment in the Chinatown alley, she expected the rocket's red glare and the clawing, greedy power she'd glimpsed then. She braced herself for roaring fury and heat from the man who'd yelled in her kitchen, the man who'd apologized for it later. She would have welcomed the burn. Gloried in it.

She hadn't expected the slow, sweet kiss he gave her. Hadn't expected him to take her under with only his lips, hadn't expected the soft touches or the single murmured word. "Stephanie."

And that, more than anything, confirmed what she'd known all along. For all that Reid Peters claimed to dislike children, for all that he pretended not to know her daughter's name, and for all that he believed his job had taken it away, there was a heart beneath his worn, battle-hardened exterior.

The man kissing her now was the man who'd sat by her bed while she lay in a coma, then wouldn't take her thanks for it afterward. He was the man who'd taken in a stray cat and worried himself over her babies. The man who'd fought to protect her and railed when it didn't seem he could.

"Reid?" There was a question in the word, and an invitation. He didn't answer out loud, but reached down and lifted her in his arms. He carried her up the stairs, and paused at her daughter's bedroom as though he'd known she would need to check one last time. As though he wanted to as well.

Then he carried her to the end of the hall, where blue moonlight streamed through the rippled glass to splash on her unmade bed. She'd never thought of her room as particularly romantic, but the high old windows gave patterns to the moonlight, the darkness—and the man who held her in his arms.

They sank together onto the old canopy bed, and when Steph put her fingers to the buttons of the ratty old lab coat, Reid stilled her with a touch and a whisper. "Leave it on."

She answered the glint in his eye and the sensuous curve of his lips with a smile of her own. She tugged at the cutoff sweatshirt. "Take it off."

And then she was free to explore the perfect chest she'd seen her daughter drooling on the other morning. He lay back and closed his eyes as she trailed her fingertips along the taut muscles of his stomach. She touched her lips to the trio of round scars that reminded him of his father, and the shallow ridge along his ribs that might have come from a knife.

The heavy muscles across his chest flexed and shifted beneath her tongue, and the moonlight gleamed off his hands, which were fisted into her sheets at his sides. Her blood beat hard and hot but it felt as though there was no rush. They had all the time in the world.

She reached up and kissed his lips, and as though that was the signal he'd been waiting for, he rolled toward her and pressed her down into the giving mattress with his good, solid weight as his hand took a slow, possessive journey down her body and his tongue delved deep and found hers.

Stephanie moaned; the soft cotton of the lab coat felt suddenly harsh as he touched her again and again through the thin barrier. Then his questing hand found the pocket slits and slid through them to stroke her hips until she was writhing beneath him and his breath was coming hard.

"Reid, please." She wasn't sure what she wanted him to do, but knew she needed something or she'd shatter from nothing more than the touch of his hand on her hip. The warm, gentle heat was closing in around them and starting to burn.

She twined her arms around his neck and poured herself into the kiss, giving him everything and asking nothing in return until he brought his arms up to cradle her and she rolled them across the soft mattress.

For the first time she blessed Jared for always getting her lab coats that were too big, because when she straddled Reid to ride the hard ridge beneath his jeans, there was room for his hands to slide beneath the white cotton and take possession of her aching, needing breasts for a slow, gentle exploration that she thought might drive her mad.

And then he was unbuttoning the coat one plastic disk at a time and spreading the halves apart so he could look at her, simply look as she rose above him and slid the coat off.

She felt beautiful. The moonlight and the man

made her beautiful, as did the sweet slide of his
hands across her flesh. The molten gold of his eyes
made her feel powerful, and when she slid down him
to press against his chest and feel, finally feel the
electric contact of skin on skin, she felt as if she'd
come awake after having been asleep her whole life.

Leaning across him, she pulled a box from the
nightstand and pressed it into his hand, figuring the
knife-sharp corners and virgin cellophane would tell
him all he needed to know.

He stood to strip out of his jeans, then stood a
moment more when she caught her breath. The
moonlight gleamed across the angle of his jaw and
the hard muscles of his chest and stomach. The
proud, arrogant jut of his member cast a blue-black
shadow against the thatch of hair and the generous
flesh below.

Apparently, Steph thought, a lack of morals hadn't
been only Luis's problem.

Then she thought no more, as Reid's weight sank
into the mattress beside her and they were finally
tangled together, naked and needy.

Had it been a year or a few days she'd been wanting this? She wasn't sure any more. She only knew
that the ache within her was building higher and
higher, and that if he wasn't inside her soon she
might scream.

He brushed a gentle hand across her breast and
she jolted, feeling every nerve ending on fire. He
kissed her deeply, probing with his tongue in the
same rhythm he set with his hand on her breast, and
she felt an answering rhythm pound within.

Wanting more, needing more, she traced a hand down his stomach and found the hard length below. He shuddered when her fingertip found the single drop of moisture at the tip. She saw his hands tremble as they slid across the cellophane, fumbling to open the box and tug a foil packet free.

All the while, she was touching him. Stroking him. Measuring him and feeling the pulse pound within her core. And then he rolled atop her, poised for the joining, with his heavy, hard bulb just teasing at the entrance. Rubbing the soft, greedy flesh that gaped open for him and wept for his entry.

Their eyes met. And held. And he slid inside her on a single slow slide that felt tight, so tight. The pressure sent ripples through her that hit the edge of her consciousness and reflected back to cross over the new ripples, increasing in intensity with the slow, urgent rhythm of his thrusts.

He whispered her name, or maybe she said his, she wasn't sure any more. She could hear nothing except the moans and the slide of flesh and the pounding of her heart in time with the breath that backed up in her lungs.

She might have climaxed once, might have climaxed a thousand times. It all built up in one steady wall of pleasure that broke over her and swept him along until she bucked up against him and held him fast with her thighs as the pulsing, pounding, throbbing pressure conquered him and he shuddered in her arms for what seemed like a year, then lay quietly. Spent.

Loved.

STEPHANIE MUST have dozed. She wasn't sure how much time passed before he left her bed. She watched him through slitted eyes as he padded to the bathroom. When he returned, he stood at the door for a long moment, watching her.

Would he leave now? Would he go home and leave his cat behind, chalking it up to a moment of exhausted weakness? Or had he finally realized that she was worth fighting the ghost of his father for? That *they* were worth fighting for.

When he crossed the room and she felt the bed dip under his weight, she felt tears prickle. When he lay on his side behind her and looped one strong arm around her waist to draw her into the tight curve of his body, she felt a single drop of wetness track down her cheek.

And when she drew his hand up to her breast and arched her back to accept the hard part of him that was pressed up against her from behind, she knew she would never be the same.

Chapter Eleven

Da-da-da-*DUM!*

When the phone woke him, Reid sat bolt upright, startled as much by the fact that he felt well rested as by the ruffled canopy above him. God. He hadn't slept that well since…he glanced down at the woman beside him, at the sleepy jade eyes that blinked in the morning light. Well, since forever.

Oh hell. He was in trouble now.

Da-da-da-*DUM!*

"I'm not answering it this time," Steph said on a yawn, sitting up and stretching as the sheet fell aside. The sight of those perfect, rosy breasts framed in soft red curls made Reid long for a paintbrush. A day off to spend in bed. Someone to tell him if he'd made the biggest mistake of his life or his best decision ever.

Da-da-da-*DUM!*

She slid out of bed when he reached for her. "Answer your phone. I'm going to check on Jilly and think about making us some breakfast."

She looped the lab coat robe over her shoulders

and sauntered down the hall and Reid felt the need
tangle in a hot, aching ball in his chest, right next to
the fear.

He scratched an itchy spot on his back and
snapped the phone open. "Peters."

"Where are you?"

Reid leapt to his feet at Sturgeon's tone. He was
rummaging for his jeans and shirt even as he answered, "Stephanie's. Why? What's wrong?"

He heard the water running in the bathroom and
glimpsed her padding down the hall to her daughter's
room.

"Stay there. Derek Bott has an alibi for the Wong
rape. He was also out of town when the phone calls
were made." Reid felt his stomach sink and a fine
tremor run through his body when Sturgeon said,
"His lawyer got him out first thing this morning."

Reid cursed, but the words were drowned out by
a scream from Jilly's room.

"My baby! Nooooo!"

Still clutching the phone, barely hearing Sturgeon
talking to midair, Reid sprinted for the hall, needing
to get to Stephanie. To Jilly.

Banishing the horrific images that flashed through
his mind, he charged into the room and slid to an
abrupt halt so he wouldn't step on the jagged shards
of broken glass.

Steph grabbed him. "She's gone! How could she
be gone? Where is she?" Her fingers clutched at his
bare forearm hard enough to leave marks. "Where
is my baby?"

A sultry breeze blew through the shattered window. The feeble glow of the dawn filtered across the rumpled white bedspread. Almond-shaped eyes peered from beneath the bed, where She Devil must have hidden her babies. Too bad she couldn't have done the same for the little girl.

Reid wrapped one arm around Steph, though he had little comfort to offer. He lifted the phone. "Sturgeon? Get over here. The kid's gone." He looked at the broken window and the rumpled bed. "And she's not in the park this time."

STEPH COULDN'T STOP shaking. Her hands shook. Her lips trembled. Her body quaked as though she'd been sitting in ice-cold water for hours. She felt numb. Too numb to cry. Too numb to scream, though her throat was raw from the screams she'd wasted before realizing they weren't going to bring her daughter back. Before realizing that she'd let the monster take her baby.

"When was the last time you saw your daughter?" The question sounded familiar, though she didn't know if it was because Sturgeon was repeating himself or if it was because she'd been asked the same questions just days earlier when Jilly had 'wandered off.'

"About ten-thirty last night. We—I checked on her and the cats…" She turned quickly toward Reid, who sat across the table with his partner, cop face firmly in place. The night might never have happened, except for a few unfamiliar aches. "Are the cats okay?"

He nodded. "They'd hidden under the bed." And that seemed the saddest irony of all. The stray cat had stayed in the house, while her Jilly—the least stray child Steph had ever known—had been taken into the night. Her lips trembled harder and she felt Reid take her hand.

She pushed it away and repeated, "I checked on her at ten-thirty. I didn't look in on her again until this morning." It had been Jilly's first night home. Why hadn't she checked on her daughter? What if she'd been afraid?

The thought brought hot, heavy tears pressing at her eyes. She'd been too wrapped up in Reid to even remember she had a daughter.

"Did you hear anything suspicious during the night?" Sturgeon asked, looking as though he'd rather be anywhere but at her kitchen table asking these questions.

"No, I was…we were…" Steph trailed off, wondering what the protocol was. Could she say, *No, I wouldn't have heard Armageddon, since your partner brought me to screaming climax no less than four times between ten-thirty and dawn?* Or perhaps, *A whole chain gang could have marched up my front steps and into my daughter's room and I wouldn't have noticed.*

"We didn't hear anything," Reid cut in, and he must've flashed Sturgeon a sign, because the other man cleared his throat, stood and mumbled something about checking on the progress of the door-to-door search before he escaped from the kitchen, leaving Steph and Reid alone.

''We'll find her,'' Reid said, patting her hand.

We'll find her. She tried to hold on to the promise, the certainty in his voice. But hope battled with the memory of clicking on Jilly's light and finding her bed empty. Feeling the air move through the broken window while the new sash lock gleamed mockingly.

Reid leaned down and kissed her soothingly on the brow, and at the touch, Steph feared she was never going to see her daughter again. She could feel it in the pressure of his lips. See it in the strain across his shoulders—and in the fact that he was wearing his shoulder holster over the freshly pressed oxford shirt Sturgeon had brought with him.

She shot to her feet. ''No! I won't let her be gone. Don't let her be gone, Reid.'' She grabbed him and ignored the flash in his eyes when she shook his arm. ''You've got to find her!''

He tried to draw her close in a soothing hug. ''We're doing our best, Steph. We're looking. We'll find her.''

''No!'' She pushed him away and pulled him close at the same time. ''It's not enough! I don't want the others looking, Reid. I want you. You have to find her for me. Please! Please?'' She wasn't sure why, but it seemed suddenly imperative that he be the one to look for her daughter. That he be the one to bring her home. To tuck her into her bed so she'd be where she belonged once again.

To follow Stephanie into her bedroom, so he'd be where he belonged as well.

She almost sat down as the strength left her legs when the delayed realization smacked her upside the head and left her reeling.

Reid had to find Jilly because he made the circle complete. He made them a family.

A family he didn't want.

He ran an impatient hand across his face and stalked across the kitchen. "There are officers out looking, I promise. Not just here, but in Chinatown, too. They've been to Derek Bott's house, but Steph..." he trailed off and looked full at her. She braced for news that couldn't be good, even as the fading glow of their new relationship battled with despair for her daughter. "We don't have much in the way of leads. We've sent a car to Bott's house, but..."

Steph knew. They had no evidence tying Bott to the crime other than DNA results from an illegal source. She sagged back into a kitchen chair. "You've got to go find her, Reid. I trust you. I love you. If you love me, you'll find my daughter."

The words she hadn't meant to speak hung in the air like an unexpected giggle in church—inappropriate and strange. Reid froze, and if he didn't physically back away, she could feel him withdraw until he was clear across the city from her, though his feet were frozen in place on her linoleum.

"Steph..." He raised his hand as though to touch her, but she leaned away and the arm dropped to his side. "I swear I'll do my best to bring her back to you."

She knew he would. It was his way, just as it was also his way to believe that he didn't want a family. That he didn't deserve one. She shook her head. "I know you will, Reid. And I'm sorry. Forget I said anything. It was just the stress talking."

But he knew her better than that. He used a finger to tilt her chin up and kissed her softly on the lips. "I'm sorry, Steph. About everything. I really am. I'll find Jilly, I promise." He kissed her again, a little deeper this time, and she could taste the goodbye.

He turned and slung his suit jacket over his shoulder on his way out the door. Steph called to him and he turned just inside the kitchen, with the light catching his mid-brown hair and painting his face until he looked as exquisitely tortured as any of the Renaissance martyrs. "Yes?"

"What about She Devil?" And they both knew she was asking about more than a cat.

He caught her eye, shook his head, and said, "She'll be happier here."

And he was gone.

REID TRIED to escape the house as quickly as he could, before he ran back into the kitchen and did something stupid like pretend for even a moment that what shouldn't have happened between Steph and him actually had a future, when it absolutely, positively didn't. Tried to escape the knowledge that he'd been sloppy in thinking the danger was over just because they had a suspect in custody.

Tried to escape knowing that a murderer had been in the house while he was making love to Stephanie, and that if they didn't find her in time, Jilly's blood would be on his hands, too.

Sturgeon grabbed his arm near the front door. "Peters."

Reid spun. "News? Did they find Jilly?" Not only were there uniforms canvassing both Patriot and Bott's neighborhood at the Chinatown/Theater border, but Maureen, Mortimer and several officers were searching the park where Jilly had been found the last time. It seemed unbelievable that she would reappear again, but Reid felt a kick of hope in his chest anyway. He wanted to find the kid so he could be done with Stephanie and the warm things she made him want.

He wanted to find the kid because he couldn't bear the thought of finding her broken and bloody in some anonymous Chinatown hotel room. He couldn't imagine never seeing the quiet little child again, not hearing her whistle that strange tune or feeling her fall asleep in his arms.

No. Strike that. He wanted to find Jilly because it was his job.

Period.

Sturgeon shook his head. "No, not yet."

"Any luck at Bott's house? With Bott?"

"That's the problem. He was with his lawyer filling out the paperwork until a half hour *after* Stephanie discovered Jilly missing.'' Reid felt a quick, hard surge of anger and frustration. Helplessness. Sturgeon offered him a mint. ''I don't know what it means. We have Bott's DNA at the two rape scenes, but he's alibied for one of them, for the calls to her house, and for this morning. It doesn't add up.''

''Not unless he can be in two places at one time,'' Reid muttered, feeling a tingle along his spine, feeling as though he was missing something. ''Which is downright impossible.''

''We're missing something,'' Sturgeon said, mirroring Reid's own thoughts. ''Let's head into Chinatown and have another look at the timelines, okay? I don't think we've overlooked anything here.''

''Yeah,'' Reid grunted, glancing quickly at the closed kitchen door, then away. ''What about her?''

Sturgeon lifted an eyebrow, but he was smart enough to keep his thoughts to himself. ''We could leave her here with her aunt and the Marine, but she understands the DNA evidence as well as anyone. Maybe we should bring her with us.''

The man in Reid didn't want to be anywhere within a mile of Stephanie. Even now, in the midst of hell on earth, he could taste her. He could feel her. He could hear her cries and smell the two of them on his own skin. And he ached.

No. The man in him didn't want to be in the same room with her for a century or so. But the cop in him knew that Sturgeon was right, so he nodded. ''You get her. I'll meet you both at the station.''

Maybe a quick detour to his place, a Brillo-and-bleach shower and another change of clothes could erase the memories long enough that he could do his job. It had been his inattention that had allowed Jilly to be snatched in the first place, so he'd damn well see her back with her mother.

He'd promised, and he'd rip his own soul out before he broke that promise.

Then again, Reid thought as he jogged down the granite steps and felt the ache in his chest, it already felt as though he had ripped out his own soul. And he wasn't sure how he was going to get it back from the red-haired, green-eyed woman who'd stolen it.

HE DIDN'T WANT to be in the room with her. Steph could sense it like a physical presence between them, chattering at her and jeering when she couldn't force herself to focus on the computer screen. "Would you go away?" she snapped at it, then winced when the words echoed out loud in the computer room.

"Problem?" Sturgeon asked from the lab desk he'd appropriated, not really looking up.

She shook her head. "Never mind." Then she reconsidered. "I was just thinking that perhaps Detective Peters would prefer to be doing something else right now."

"Why?" Peters snapped as he spun and paced back to the window and glared down at the streets of Chinatown. "I'm fine. There's nothing to be done until we have another name. If it's not Bott, it has to be someone." He reached over one shoulder to scratch the middle of his back. "You got anything, Sturgeon? Any names?"

For the third time since they'd ridden up to the thirteenth floor together in the too-small elevator, Reid spoke to his partner as though he thought the DNA evidence was played out. Steph bristled. "It's Bott. He did it."

Reid shot her a look that left her steaming. "According to the law, it's not. He has an alibi for three of the incidents. It can't be him."

"The law is wrong," she practically snarled, and pointed at the computer screen, where the DNA match between the rape kits and Derek Bott's DNA—which she had illegally scanned and inputted into the Boston General system—was shown in clear black and white. "The DNA is a match."

"It can't be," he shot back. "And arguing that it is won't get your daughter back!"

The words echoed.

Peters cursed and scratched absently at his chest as he walked over to her computer chair. "I'm sorry."

She spun away from him, trying not to remember how vulnerable he'd looked crouched on her sofa with his head in his hands. How they'd moved together in the night. How they'd loved each other. She crossed her arms. "Don't be sorry. And don't be mad at me because you're too much of a coward to take a chance on us. Be mad at yourself." Aware of Sturgeon staring furiously at the drift of creased index cards he'd poured onto the desk he'd taken over, she glared out the window, seeing nothing. "Scratch that. Don't be mad at anyone. Just do your job. Find my daughter and you can go back to your empty apartment with your dead fake plants and your empty brown life. Okay, Peters? I don't care what you do next. Just find my daughter."

He cursed. "I'm trying, Steph. We're all trying, but we need more to go on. Until we've got something, we'll just be knocking on random doors, asking the same old questions. Don't you see that?"

Steph saw, but she didn't care. "You promised, Reid. You promised to find my daughter. Don't add liar to your life list under the words *emotional coward.*"

She thought he might snap back at that, might give her the fight she needed, but he didn't. He merely turned and walked back to the window and looked out. She didn't think he saw anything, either. He whistled a fragment of melody and her throat closed.

It was what she'd come to think of as Jilly's song, the poignant string of notes the little girl had been whistling for days now. Steph wondered whether she was whistling now. Whether she was cold. Hungry. Afraid.

Alive.

She choked back a sob and stared hard at the computer screen, willing the tears away. When that didn't work, she surged to her feet and stumbled out into the carpeted hallway, past the cop who'd taken over the receptionist's desk, and down the bright corridor to the ladies' room. She heard Reid calling her, but she didn't stop until she was in the farthest stall, retching miserably.

She heard the bathroom door open, then shut again, and she hoped whoever it was would have the good sense to leave her alone. There was a fifty-fifty chance that she'd slug them or cry on them, and she didn't have the energy for either.

"Hey." The voice was quiet, but unmistakably that of the man who'd sat at her bedside waiting for her to wake up from that coma a year ago—not because he needed her to name her attacker, but because he cared whether she woke up or not.

At least that's what she'd told herself. But if he was too stubborn and too committed to beating himself up over a childhood he hadn't been able to control, too stuck in his belief that a Chinatown cop like him couldn't find a way to balance love and family against the job, then it didn't really matter whether he cared or not.

Because he didn't care enough.

"Go away," she whimpered, sliding down to sit on the cold floor tiles, feeling the chill seep through her jeans and wishing she'd worn a lab coat. Then she thought of the gleam in Reid's eyes when he'd taken the lab coat off her the night before, and was glad she hadn't.

"Sorry. Can't do that either." He hunkered down beside her on the ladies' room floor and took her hand. Squeezed it. "I'm sorry, Steph. Sorry about all of it. If I'd been paying better attention last night…"

On a quick, vividly sensual memory, she shook

her head. "Don't beat yourself up over it. We thought we were safe last night. We thought it was Bott." She glanced up at the ceiling tiles and pictured the matching DNA patterns marching side by side down the gel. Identical. "Damn it, it *is* Bott. I don't care about the alibis."

"Unfortunately, the District Attorney does."

Steph felt herself relax fractionally against Reid's side, felt his warmth battle the chill of the floor and felt the good, steady pulse of blood through his body. Saw it in the throb of a pulse at his throat. And found a smile. "Then the D.A.'s a fool."

"You have no idea, sweetheart." Reid sighed. "Unfortunately, until we can explain to him how Derek Bott could be in two places at once, we're stuck. And the uniforms at the Bott house aren't even sure where he is right now, so we're double stuck because we don't have the authority to find him and we're not sure what to charge him with if we could." He cursed and wiggled against the wall, scratching his back against the rough tile. "I still feel like we're missing something. Like it's right there, only not. Know what I mean?"

Steph nodded. "I know. But short of Derek being in two places at once..." She frowned. "Well, actually we don't need him in two places at the same time. We just need his DNA in one of those places."

Reid snorted. "An enemy framing him with a planted DNA sample? That's something that only happens in the movies." He shifted again on the hard floor, then stood with a grunt. "You ready to go back? We should see if the others have found anything."

Wearily, aching in unexpected places, both from their lovemaking the night before and from the toll the last few days had taken, Steph heaved herself to her feet and rinsed her mouth out with tinny Boston tap water.

Walking back through the sterile white corridor with Reid at her side, she frowned. "No, not a plant. You're right, we're missing something." A tarantula of black lines and boxes crept across her mind. Something in the pedigree?

When they reached the computer room—which was starting to feel like the center of a besieged castle—Steph pulled up the half-drawn Bott family tree. It was incomplete, as they only had information on two of Sinclair Bott's children. She traced her finger along the lines of descent. "How can Bott's DNA be in two places at once?" she asked rhetorically, but Reid answered her from across the room.

"Not possible, unless he has a clone." He grinned crookedly at her. "And from what I know of the state of the art around here, you're still a few years away from that."

Steph froze, staring at the angled lines connecting Sinclair Bott to his brother in a relationship that was closer than a normal sibling's. "Not a clone," she breathed, only barely aware that the detectives had hustled to their feet at the tone in her voice, only barely aware that her finger trembled as it pointed to Derek Bott's father…and his twin brother. "An identical twin."

Reid swore quickly, explosively. Then cursed himself again. "I saw children in the house when we took Bott. Identical boys."

Sturgeon was already on the phone when Steph lifted her eyes to Reid's. "You said once that crime runs in families around here. I guess in this family it runs more closely than in others. You said it yourself. Bad blood."

Reid closed his eyes, bit back another useless curse, and nodded tightly. "We knew Derek had brothers. We never thought to ask about a twin." He swore aloud. "That's why the patterns weren't falling into place. There are two different perps hiding behind each other." He glanced out the window, down to the maze of Chinatown thirteen stories below. "And they've been setting up the alibis so we couldn't get a conviction to stick on either one."

He strode to the wipe board at the back of the computer room and uncapped a pen. Sturgeon joined him, still barking a string of instructions into the phone.

"The first set of rapes fit together. Teenage streetwalkers. Violent. No DNA." Reid listed the names, and Steph shuddered to see them written out. "But Mae Wong didn't fit. She was the wrong age and there was DNA at the scene." He wrote the child's name at the top of another column.

"Honey's death fit the first pattern. She was a streetwalker and there was no semen, though there was DNA beneath her fingernails," Sturgeon said and Reid wrote the name in the first column.

"Then the letter bomb. That was way off pattern, and didn't fit within the blackmail scheme Bott had going with Stephanie." He wrote it under the second column. "I think the date rape was a learning experience. After one of them was hauled up on charges, they learned about the DNA and took care not to leave it again.''

"Until Mae Wong," Sturgeon pointed out and they both stared at the board while a pattern emerged.

Finally.

Steph stepped forward, though she didn't want to be anywhere near the two neat columns. She gestured at the first column. "That one is the thinker. The planner. The smart one." They all gazed at the second column. "And his brother wants to be just like him, but he's not bright enough. He leaves DNA behind and compromises both of them. He plans a bomb that does nothing but confuse the issue.''

Reid nodded. "The second brother probably did the setup in Jilly's room with the teddy bear and the model horses. There was something childish about it.''

"But the first brother used the scenario to bring Peters in with Honey Moreplease." Sturgeon flipped his phone open again. "Makes sense. The DNA confused us by pointing to one perp when there were two all along.''

"But where does Jilly fit in?" Steph demanded. "And why is he still after us when I can't help him any more? Revenge? Is he trying to get back at me for turning this over to the police, even though he brought Reid in? That doesn't make sense!'' Her voice was rising as the fear rose again at the question she couldn't ask.

What column did Jilly belong in?

Reid and Sturgeon stood shoulder to shoulder in their matching police-issue holsters and Steph felt the screams push at the back of her throat at the knowledge in their eyes.

"We don't think he's worried about the DNA any more, Stephanie." Sturgeon's eyes were kind but Reid's were hard and cold. Cop's eyes. Angry eyes. The older detective continued, "Bringing Reid in with the Moreplease murder didn't make any sense if he was still hoping to avoid capture. We think he was playing with you. He's become fixated on you and your daughter. He doesn't care about the DNA any more. He wants you."

Steph felt her knees turn to water and Reid caught her on the way down. He helped her to a chair and tipped the dregs of a bottle of water into her mouth until she coughed and batted him away, feeling as though her whole world was crashing down around her as Sturgeon moved and wrote a single word below and between the two columns.

Jilly.

"They've both got her," Reid grated, rising and pacing to the window and back. "And we need to find her. Fast."

The unspoken words echoed in the computer room.

Or else.

Chapter Twelve

Having a name should have made things easier, Reid thought fiercely. Having two names should have doubled the speed of their investigation.

They had pictures of the Botts. Or else they had two pictures of the same Bott. It was hard to tell but Reid had convinced himself he could see the difference in their eyes. One pair were slightly vacant. Confused.

The other had eyes like a snake. Cold. Dead. Elemental.

But five hours later, they still didn't have Derek Bott. They didn't have his identical twin brother Dwayne.

And they didn't have Jilly. Time was running out. He could feel it. She was still out there, somewhere. He had to believe that, because the alternative was unacceptable.

With a little girl's life at stake, D.A. Hedlund had come through with the arrest warrants in record time. Derek's wife Maria and her twin sons were pinned down as tight as the Chinatown officers could get them. Patriot was watching Stephanie's house as well as Mortimer's place, but there hadn't been any activity in that neighborhood all day.

There wasn't much going on in Chinatown, either. Reid stared down the thirteen stories and watched a narrow parade of cars snake down Kneeland Street in front of the Boston General Genetic Research Building. Ten minutes ago there had been a fender bender, and the cabby and the other motorist were coming to blows over insurance cards.

From this high up, they looked like ants.

"Anything?"

He glanced up at Stephanie's quiet question, and had to stop himself from smoothing the tired smudges beneath her eyes with his thumb. He didn't have the right to touch her. Didn't want the right.

Liar.

He shook his head. "Nothing. For better or worse, most of what we do is hurry up and wait." He gave in to the urge, and touched her cheek. "You could try to nap in your boss's office. I seem to remember she keeps a cot in there."

Steph shook her head, knotted and reknotted her fingers. "I can't settle down. Too much caffeine, I guess." She shifted from one foot to the other, and glanced down at the street. Her expression lightened slightly when she saw the fight in progress. "When things are slow with the experiments, we spend time watching the street. It's like television except you never know what program will be on. Some weeks there are two or three grease fires in the Chinese restaurants, other weeks none. We see the accidents and the traffic jams and we're so happy to be above it all in our ivory tower. Then the day's over and we go back down there and rejoin the masses. So many people."

Reid saw her brow knit as she stared out the big picture window, and knew that she was trying to see her daughter in one of the tiny buildings spread out below them. He gave her a quick one-armed hug and let her go before her scent could draw him closer. Tempt him.

"Then go for a walk and burn off some of the twitches." It was on the tip of his tongue to offer to walk with her, but that would be unwise in the extreme. Not just because Sturgeon needed him at the lab, which had remained their impromptu command central even after the DNA mystery had been solved, but because something deep within him needed to go for that walk. With her.

Impossible. He needed to be on the job. He had to *be* the job. He'd already proven that when he let Stephanie distract him from it, terrible things happened.

Little girls disappeared.

So he waved to the young officer sitting at the receptionist's desk in the lobby. "O'Connell. Walk with Miss Alberts, will you? She's going to stretch her legs." He fixed the rookie with a stare. "Nothing seedy and stay off the Commons. If you see the suspect or you feel like something's off, come right back here, no questions asked, got it?"

Stephanie huffed, "I'm not stupid and I don't need a keeper, Peters," but he stared O'Connell down until the kid gulped and nodded.

"Yes, sir."

With a snort, Stephanie grabbed her purse and stomped off toward the elevators. Reid held O'Connell back long enough to whisper, "Anything happens to her and you're dead, got it?"

The rookie stammered an affirmative that had Sturgeon snickering from his desk as the lobby doors closed. "That one's scared right out of his uniform now. Good job, Peters. He'll be drawing down on some poor hotdog vendor now, trying to protect her."

"Fine. Just as long as he catches sight of Bott, too."

Sturgeon cocked an eyebrow and slid his mint from his left cheek to his right. "You think either Bott is going to show?"

Reid shook his head. "Nah. I think they're holed up tight, trying to decide what the hell to do next. We should've had a demand called in to the house by now." And that, more than anything, worried Reid to death. What if they hadn't called for ransom because they had nothing to trade?

No. Jilly was alive. He could feel it. He just hoped she stayed that way long enough to get found.

"The officers in Patriot haven't heard a peep," Sturgeon said unnecessarily. He glanced down at the street, then back to Reid. "You sure you want to walk away after we find Jilly and get the Botts?"

The change of subject was not welcome.

Reid bared his teeth. "Mind your own business, Sturgeon. Just because the white picket fence and water-park thing works for you doesn't mean it works for cops in general."

"Who says it works?" Sturgeon asked as he unwrapped another mint and popped it home. "A marriage doesn't run itself and it's a damn bit of effort to keep it on track, especially when you go to work and see the things we see."

It was the first time Sturgeon had ever admitted to Reid that he felt the job, too. He always seemed untouched by the mayhem. Unperturbed by the atrocity. Reid shrugged. "Then why do it?" He meant the family, not the job, and Sturgeon understood. The job was a given for both of them.

"Because for all the work, going home to Jen at the end of a filthy day is a damn sight better than going home to a cat and a house full of dead silk plants."

The phone rang and Reid almost jumped out of his skin. Sturgeon was closest, so he answered it. Nodded once. Smiled grimly.

He folded the phone and handed Reid his suit coat. "They just called her house with a demand."

"Which was?"

Sturgeon paused in the act of gathering his index cards. "We were right. They want Steph, too. Or rather *he* does." Talking with Derek Bott's lawyer and a few acquaintances from the neighborhood had told them that Derek Bott was typical lowlife, but that his brother Dwayne was different.

The locals didn't have anything bad to say out loud about Dwayne. Their eyes said it for them.

Dwayne was scary bad. And he had Jilly.

Reid snarled as they jogged to the elevators. "Give me some good news, why don't you?"

Sturgeon grinned and stabbed the down button. "We got a trace."

WHEN SHE HIT the pavement outside the Genetic Research Building, Steph was surprised that she didn't see anyone she knew—until she remembered it was Sunday. How could it be Sunday? The weekend was such a normal thing that it seemed it shouldn't have come when so many things were topsy-turvy in her world.

"Ma'am? Are you okay?" The young officer hovered at her elbow, and Steph noticed the looks she was getting from the passing tourists. They were probably wondering what she'd done wrong.

Then again, she was still trying to figure out the same thing.

She brushed him off and started to walk, not being at all particular about the direction. She just needed to walk. She needed to do something, anything, other than sit in the computer room for one more minute breathing the same air as Detective Reid Peters.

Coward. He was a coward for turning away from what they could have together. She ground her teeth and concentrated on the anger, since it was easier than thinking about Jilly as she stalked along the Chinatown streets, shadowed by a rookie who looked barely past puberty.

Caught up in her fury, she walked faster.

"Ma'am?" The rookie's voice interrupted. "We should turn back now. We're getting out of Chinatown and I don't want to get in trouble with Detective Peters." The kid said Reid's name as if he was a god, and it irked Steph so much she didn't admit that they'd already walked farther than she'd intended.

"So go back yourself if the umbilical cord doesn't stretch into the Theater District." She knew it was mean, but she was feeling mean, and because of it she ducked into the next crummy alley she saw, scowling as the officer swore and followed.

Then she slowed, ashamed. When O'Connell caught up, she shrugged. "Sorry about that. I just…" She shook her head. "I don't know. Never mind. We can go back whenever you want."

"Appreciate it." The fair-haired rookie gestured her to the other end of the alley, which opened onto an off-off Washington Street side road that Steph rarely ventured down. There were smaller theaters with tired-looking signs and burned-out bulbs mixed in amongst greasy gray doors that led to the apartment buildings lurking high above the street.

Steph and her shadow walked quickly toward the end of the road, where they could see the welcome Kneeland Street cross traffic. It was amazing that they were only a few blocks from both Patriot and

Boston General, yet the light seemed to have been sucked away from the street, leaving it drab and lifeless.

They passed a small crowd milling outside a theater. The sagging wooden marquee that arched above the door and sprawled across the building next door advertised a matinee of a "New Smash Hit" Steph had never heard of. She was just letting O'Connell drag her past the crowd when the doors were thrown open and music spilled out onto the street.

She gasped.

It was Jilly's song.

The notes were so simple that a child could whistle them. A child *had* whistled them. And how could she have learned them when she'd never been here before? Steph stopped dead, losing the melody when the small crowd of ticket holders surged through the tired doors and disappeared.

"Ma'am? Ms. Alberts? We need to keep moving. This isn't the safest part of town." O'Connell was practically dancing in his urgency, but Steph shook her head.

"No, you don't understand. That song…" She gestured toward the "New Smash Hit" sign.

"Pretty awful, I agree. I don't think you'll have to worry about the show pushing out its rivals on the main drag. Shall we go?"

She spun and headed for the theater. "My daughter has been whistling that song for three days now. Ever since she was taken the first time."

He might be a rookie, but O'Connell was neither

dumb nor as pliable as he seemed. Steph made it only a few steps into the street when he grabbed her by the arm, swung her into a busted-out doorway and blocked her with his body, swearing as he fumbled for his radio. When Steph tried to push past him and reach the street again, he barked, "Stay!"

She subsided. "I'm not a dog. And who do you think you are, anyway?"

He scowled. "The rookie whose butt is on the line if anything happens to you or your daughter." When she continued to struggle, he softened his tone but not his hold on her arm. "Think for a minute, Ms. Alberts. If your daughter was kept in or near that theater—because we can assume that terrible music isn't being played anywhere else in the city—then how are you helping things by crashing in there right now?"

Seeing reason where she didn't want to, Steph nodded curtly. "Then you go in and get her."

"Why don't we both stay here and wait for backup? Or better yet, since a uniform huddled in a doorway isn't exactly normal for this neighborhood, why don't we keep walking right around the block?"

While he called in a report, Steph had to admit the logic of the plan. She didn't like it, but he was right.

"Ready?" O'Connell, towheaded and earnest, took her arm, ushered her out of the doorway and started marching her toward Kneeland Street, careful to keep his body between her and the street.

The first bullet caught him high on the shoulder.

The first of the shrill childish screams turned Steph's guts to water as the officer fell.

And without thinking, she ran across the street toward her daughter.

Chapter Thirteen

"Christ. Can't we get a bulldozer out here or something?" Reid complained as Sturgeon blipped the siren and leaned on the horn. Cars were snarled all around them, trying and failing to find a way around the fresh collision that stretched across Kneeland Street just before the Theater District. "There's nowhere for them to go except onto the sidewalks." And he'd swear that the cab involved in the accident up ahead was the same one he'd watched have a fender bender not a half hour earlier.

"The other unit's stuck on the far side of Theater, and some of their boys are meeting us at the trace address. They'll keep it quiet until we get there. We've got time. Bott wouldn't have called to arrange the exchange if they didn't have her."

But the words rang false. Sturgeon and Reid both knew that plenty of kidnappers collected on dead bodies. And the very thought of Stephanie exchanging herself for her daughter was enough to make him want to shoot something.

Or someone. Dwayne Bott would do nicely.

The radio on the dash spluttered to life and Reid's chest tightened when he heard O'Connell's voice. His whole body began to tingle. To itch, right above his heart. Then he understood the transmission and his heart stopped.

Stephanie was in the Theater District. She was across the street from the apartment building where Derek and Dwayne Bott were holding Jilly.

Hell.

He was out of the car in an instant, heard Sturgeon yelling his name but he didn't turn back as he lit out at a dead run toward the accident. The cross street O'Connell had named was two blocks up.

He didn't see the rookie and redheaded woman emerge to circle around the block as they had planned. Didn't see the backup in place. He didn't see anything. He cursed, leapt over a tangled piece of taxicab and sprinted for the Theater District, praying he wouldn't be too late.

NOT HEARING Jilly screaming any more, but still feeling the awful wails deep within her bones, Steph crept up the sagging stairs and wondered what the hell she was doing. Backup. She should be waiting for backup. For the police. For Reid.

No. She wouldn't think of him now. And she wouldn't wait. Jilly needed her.

The stairwell was quiet, but muffled noises filtered in from one landing above her. She'd seen movement from the third floor just before Officer O'Connell had fallen. She thought he was alive. She knew she should have stayed with him, but nothing was more important than getting Jilly back.

Nothing.

Her purse bumped against her side as Steph eased her way up the last set of stairs and wished she had a weapon. She thought of her pepper spray, fumbled the silver canister free and left the purse behind as she stepped into the second-floor hallway. Voices rose from an open door on the left.

"I can't believe you shot the cop. Jesus, Dwayne. Like we're not in enough trouble already? What the hell were you thinking?" The voice was almost cracking with stress, but Steph thought it could have been the voice of her threatening caller.

"First off, we're in trouble because of you, brother, and don't you forget it. And besides, we've got a plan, remember?" This voice, too, could have been that of Steph's caller.

She supposed that in a way they both were. Easing one foot in front of the other, she eased down the hallway until she was just outside the door.

"I don't understand why we can't just leave. We should just get out of here like Sinclair said to do." Though the voices were superficially identical, the whiny, stressed undertones told Steph that it was the first speaker, Derek. She hoped they kept talking.

"Not without the woman. She owes me." This voice was cold. Unyielding. Deadly.

Dwayne.

Steph felt a shiver crawl up her back at the inflection and very much wanted to curl up in a ball until it all went away. But she couldn't. Jilly was in there, and she wasn't going to let her daughter down again.

"And the kid?"

"She's not important. We'll kill her on our way out and dump her in the Charles. No need to leave anything behind."

She must've made a noise at that, because there was a sudden silence from within the room. A shuffling. Not willing to wait for them to come find her, she stepped into the sagging doorway, grappling with a half-formed, half-baked plan that wasn't much of a plan at all. The pepper spray was tucked into her waistband at the small of her back like she'd seen Reid do with his gun. It gave her a small sense of security.

Very small.

"You!" One of the men spluttered, and the faint whine identified him as Derek even as his spitting image smiled cruelly and said, "So, you've decided to join us, have you?" from across the room. "Clever girl."

Dwayne walked toward her on long, powerful legs. His thick dark hair looked oily, and his mouth was twisted in a mocking line.

Fear shivered through Stephanie, but she held herself still as he twisted a lock of her hair between his fingers and smiled. "What are you doing here, Stephanie?" He'd never said her name before. Now, it sent tarantulas of dread spreading through her body until she thought she might faint. No. She mustn't. She had to get to Jilly. "Come to say you're sorry for not following instructions the first time? Come to make it up to my brother and me?'' Dwayne licked his lips suggestively and rubbed that lock of her hair against his cheek.

Steph shuddered and didn't bother to hide it. ''I came to get my daughter.''

She wasn't surprised when they laughed.

''Why would we give away our little girl? She's pretty.'' Dwayne licked his lips. ''And Derek likes them young.'' Another, bigger shudder worked its way through Steph and she bit her lip to keep from screaming.

''I want to see my daughter.''

The plan was simple. She would do whatever it took to keep Jilly alive until Reid came for them. And he *would* come. She knew it. She trusted him. Whether he was the job or the man, he was Reid, and he'd rescue them.

She only hoped he made it in time.

''Of course you want to see your daughter, Stephanie.'' Dwayne snapped his fingers. ''Search her and put her in with the kid.'' He walked to the window and idly picked up a rifle that had been leaning against the wall. ''Take a moment to say goodbye to her, okay? Sinclair Jr. should be out back any minute with the car. We'll just slip through the theater and *poof,*'' he snapped his fingers, ''we'll be gone.''

Steph whimpered and his eyes slid over to her. ''How would you like to be Mrs. Bott? There won't be any ceremony, of course, but I think you'll do quite nicely for the both of us.''

Tears stung her eyes but she held them in check as she thought furiously. She sucked her stomach in and felt the pepper spray slide out of her waistband and drop into her jeans where it wedged down low. Derek liked little girls. Maybe he wouldn't search her too carefully.

"Let me see my daughter and I'll be whatever you want."

"Don't worry. You will anyway," Dwayne said, and motioned for his brother to take her away. As she was dragged through a door between the faded couch and the chipped, yellowed kitchen, she saw Dwayne shoulder the rifle and squeeze off a few rounds down into the street, and she shut her eyes at the reports.

Reid. O'Connell.

Jilly.

Steph felt her heart try to beat its way out of her chest when she saw the little girl curled up high in a corner of the bed, weeping soundlessly. She barely felt Derek's bruising hands on her body as he gave her a disinterested, sloppy search and missed the pepper spray wedged in her jeans.

"Jilly!"

The little form uncurled instantly and sprang at Steph, wailing, "Mama!"

Steph gathered her daughter up, shaking almost as hard as Jilly was, and hugged her, whispering that she loved her, that she was safe now, that everything was going to be okay.

Then she heard the door shut and the key turn in

the lock. And the crack of the high-powered rifle and the men's cheer, and Dwayne's voice calling, "Hey Stephanie! I just got myself a cop. I think he's a friend of yours." A flurry of rifle shots.

She buried her face in Jilly's hair.

Reid.

He wasn't coming for them. Maybe he couldn't. She'd deal with that later.

Right now she needed to get Jilly to safety.

SLIPPING ALONG the edges of one of the shabbiest roads in the Theater District, Reid saw a man crouched down in the shadows of a doorway opposite the building where the trace had identified an apartment on the third floor. The number was registered to Dwayne Tobb, which Reid thought was an unimaginative alias.

Unfortunately, it had been effective. It hadn't popped up on any of their searches.

"It's me," the figure hissed, and Reid lowered his weapon and joined O'Connell. The officer was alone. And bleeding. "Get down, he's shooting out the window."

Having already heard the report over the radio, Reid merely crouched down beside the rookie. "Where's Steph?" He would've grabbed the rookie and shaken him for letting her run into danger, but he saw the red leaking between O'Connell's fingers from a wound in his upper chest. He heard the wet, sucking breaths that spoke of a collapsing lung and saw another wound high on his thigh.

There was a crack and both men ducked as a bullet whistled past the bare shelter of the doorway and smacked into rotting wooden frame at eye level. The shot was followed by several more, and Reid felt one crease his upper arm.

He shrank farther into the alcove and clapped a hand to the shallow gash. "Where is she?" he repeated to the rookie, whose eyes were starting to roll.

"She went in, Detective. I'm sorry. I couldn't stop her. He started shooting and the kid screamed...I couldn't stop her. I'm sorry."

The fear congealed, cold and hard and greedy in Reid's gut and the rage flared until he had to stop himself from shaking the rookie until his teeth rattled and his other lung collapsed. He resisted the need to yell that O'Connell shouldn't have let her walk this way, especially shouldn't have let her take this street. That he should've gotten her away the moment she heard the music, that he should've dragged her to safety even after he was shot.

But he didn't, because none of it could be undone. None of it could have been predicted. Things happened. Parents fought. Children were caught in crossfire. Hookers died on cheap motel sheets. Reid could hate the people who made such things happen, he could devote his life to stopping them, but he couldn't fix everything.

He could fix his own life, though. He could take the things he wanted and fight to make them work. He could love Stephanie and Jilly and make a family with them if he tried hard enough.

If he got them out of this alive.

So he gave the pale rookie a man-to-man nod, wadded his suit jacket against the hole in the kid's chest and directed him to press on it. "Backup's en route." Assuming it ever got through that accident, or managed to backtrack far enough around to come in another way. "Which door?"

O'Connell gestured with his chin. "Sagging green one next to the ticket office. Third window over, I think. The one with the old theater marquee right below it."

The marquee in question looked as though it might let go and crash the three stories to the ground at any moment. Reid scowled. He could picture the inside— a warren of narrow, smelly hallways and cramped, smelly rooms. Sort of like his place.

Then he froze as he saw a window above the marquee slide open. Saw a leg appear. And saw Stephanie, with her daughter balanced carefully on her hip, ease her way out the window and take a shaky step along the rotting wood.

"Jesus." He didn't dare yell, for fear of attracting the Botts' attention to their escaping prisoners. Didn't dare wave her back from an inevitable fall for the same reason.

Did she realize how precarious her perch was? Perhaps so, and she had decided the alternative was worse. She was inching her way along the false theater front, aiming for a rusty, crusty fire escape at the far end of the building.

She couldn't possibly see that a three-foot section

between her and the fire escape was supported by nothing. The decorative cross members and bracing lay in sharp-edged heap on the sidewalk, and the few boards that remained sagged into empty space.

"Radio Sturgeon and get him here," Reid snapped at the groggy O'Connell. "I don't care if he drives on the sidewalk or straight through a department store to get here, just get him here. Got it?"

Without waiting for the rookie's assent, Reid yanked his weapon free and charged across the street, dodging and weaving, hoping to foul the shooter's aim. A pair of shots chipped the asphalt at his heels. He'd just reached the faded green door when he heard the sound he'd been dreading.

It wasn't the sound of rotting wood giving way beneath the woman he loved and the child he wanted for his own.

It was the slide of a second window and a man's voice yelling, "Hey, you. Stop! Hey, Dwayne. They're out on the ledge. They're getting away!"

Don't look down. Don't look back. The words had become Steph's mantra as she edged her way along the soft boards that had once supported a sign for Coming Attractions. Yeah, she thought, coming soon, the amazing Stephanie and Jilly Alberts and their death-defying midair walk.

No. Can't think of that now. Her foot wobbled on the one sturdy beam she'd found and Steph closed her eyes for a quick moment and used the feel of her daughter in her arms to find her balance once again.

There were no "do-overs" here. She had one chance and one chance only. But when she'd pressed her ear to the bedroom door—flimsy enough to hear through but not so flimsy that she could break it if she could think of some way to overpower the men on the other side—she'd heard Dwayne say, "It's time to cut our losses and scram, brother. We can't stay here anymore. I can't alibi you out of this mess and you can't alibi me. Got it?"

"And those two?"

"We'll take the woman and dump the kid, just like we planned."

And she'd known she couldn't afford to get into their getaway car. The police wouldn't be able to find her then, and she didn't think a can of pepper spray would be enough to hold off Dwayne Bott, who seemed more than human to her.

More than evil.

Escape was her only option.

The window had been locked with a simple bolt, making it a suitable prison for a little girl, but not for a grown woman. That is, until the grown woman looked down at the spongy, rotten ledge and the street three stories below.

But there had been no other choice. It was the Botts or the ledge.

Don't look down. Don't look back. She was almost halfway to freedom when she heard the sash scrape behind her, heard Derek's excited shout.

And she started to run toward the fire escape.

REID DIDN'T BOTHER with stealth. The woman he loved was up there with Dwayne and Derek Bott and she needed him.

He didn't wait for backup. He simply charged up the stairs and flung himself into the room where the brothers Bott had holed up.

"Freeze! Police!" Have to remember there's two of them, he reminded himself as he flattened his back to a thin wall and tried to cover them both at once. It was a little disconcerting that they looked exactly alike as they advanced toward him, like he was in a funhouse hall of mirrors, only this was no fun.

Then one snapped, "Go get the woman and the girl. I'll take care of him."

The dead snake eyes told Reid he was facing the smarter, meaner brother. "Dwayne. You don't want to do this." The high-powered rifle in Bott's hands was designed more for sniper shots like the one that had felled O'Connell than it was for close-range combat, but Reid figured it could put a pretty big hole in him regardless. "This doesn't have to be as bad as you'll make it if you kill me."

Bott snorted. "Don't play me, detective. You've got us on a bunch of rapes, murder, kidnapping, shooting that cop in the street, and who knows what the hell else? It can't possibly get any worse for Derek."

"But you did most of that, Dwayne. Not Derek." Reid was agonizingly aware that Derek Bott was crawling out the window after Steph and Jilly. But Dwayne's finger was hard on the rifle trigger and

Reid wouldn't be much help if he got shot in the process of taking Dwayne out. The anger soared and he fought it. He needed logic now, not rage. He needed a distraction.

The big man shrugged. "Who cares? Derek will go down for all of it. I'll see to that. The DNA will match. I'll make sure his alibis recant, then I'll disappear for good. He screwed up in the first place, raping that little kid without a condom, and I've had to do all this work to get him out of it. Then he got cute with that letter bomb and the teddy bear...." Dwayne blew out a frustrated breath. "Frankly, he's a liability at this point."

Reid developed an odd feeling on the back of his neck. Not an itch that told him something was wrong, but a prickling that told him there was someone there. Someone friendly.

Do something, Sturgeon, he thought, *I'm running out of time here.*

"Oh, damn—!" The muffled shout came from outside the window. There was a spongy crackling, and the whole building seemed to sway for an instant under an onslaught of furious popping and tearing sounds. Reid heard Stephanie scream and thought his heart had stopped.

Dwayne half turned toward the window and bellowed his twin's name, and that break was enough for Reid. He dove on the heavier man, swinging the rifle away and down. A shot rang out as it discharged through the floor and into the—he hoped—empty apartment below.

Reid pistol-whipped Bott, who sagged and howled, but fought back with the strength and ferocity of a grizzly. He grabbed Reid in a bear hug that threatened to crack a few ribs, and carried him toward the window.

"Bott! Freeze!" And suddenly there were men pouring into the tiny gray apartment, surrounding Bott and yelling for him to let Reid go. To surrender.

Reid punched Dwayne hard in the face and felt the contact sing up his arm and meet the anger that burned within him. The big man sagged and Reid hit the floor running, praying to a God he barely remembered from childhood that some of the marquee had survived the collapse. He stuck his head out the window and looked out.

Nothing.

A jumble of wood, girders, and smashed neon lights lay strewn across the street. A human figure was sprawled atop it. Unmoving. A spreading pool of dark radiated from the still figure.

Uniforms and rescue workers were gathered around the mess, gesturing and pointing, and Reid scanned the wreck frantically, hoping to see a woman and a child standing at the edges of the disaster area, or maybe being treated in the back of the ambulance, or—

"Reid." The whisper came from his left and he whipped around to stare.

She was standing not ten feet away from him, balanced on a shattered spike of beam that hadn't yet fallen. Jilly's arms were wrapped hard around her neck and there were tears in both their eyes. As he watched, Stephanie's fingers went limp and a shiny silver canister spun through the air and fell to the ground, three stories away.

Jilly's little lips formed the whispered word, "Tek-tif," and Reid felt his heart lurch.

Then it stopped when he heard a crackling sound and the beam started to let go.

FROM THE MOMENT she'd pepper-sprayed Derek Bott and seen him reel back and fall and heard his choked-off scream when he hit bottom…from the moment she'd seen the rest of the fragile structure break free and follow Bott down three stories of open air, Steph had known it was only a matter of time before she and Jilly followed.

She could see no way out. There were scurrying, yelling figures below, but she knew any sort of landing site they might rig would be too late. The heavy ironwork and sharp boards below were too dangerous.

But perhaps, she'd thought, she could curl herself tightly enough around Jilly to protect the little girl from the landing.

Maybe she could save her daughter.

Then Reid had leaned his head out the window, and all thoughts of martyrdom fled. She *wanted* to live, damn it, if only so she'd have the opportunity to try once more to prove to Reid that he wasn't like his father. That he wasn't just a cop. That he'd make a good daddy. A good husband.

That he deserved a family.

He didn't look at her right away, but instead stared down at the mess below. At the broken body of Derek Bott. She whispered, "Reid," as though a yell would bring her precious foothold tumbling down, and his head whipped around. His eyes bored into hers, and she felt the tears rise. She let the pepper spray go and heard it land on the street far below.

So close. He was so close, yet the ten feet seemed like miles. And the fragment of beam she was clinging to with all her might began to give way.

"Rope," he barked over his shoulder. "I need rope. Belts, anything, and I mean *now!*" She could hear the scuffling behind him and was grateful that he wasn't alone with Dwayne. Wasn't shot dead, though she saw the blood on his arm and his face and knew he hadn't escaped unscathed.

"Reid," she whispered again, afraid that even breathing too deeply would send her and her daughter crashing down. "You'll have to catch Jilly."

She saw the knowledge in his eyes, knew that the momentum would be too much for her perch but she could see no other way. But damn it, she wanted to live. She wanted to love him, whether he liked it or not.

She could see willing hands holding his belt and legs as Reid began to inch his way out the window, following the scant remnant of scaffolding that had survived the collapse. He ran out of support after only a few feet.

He reached out toward her and she knew. He could go no farther.

''I love you,'' she said, not whispering now because the beam was cracking anyway, and she saw the answering emotion gleaming gold in the afternoon light.

''I love you, too, Steph. And by God, I'm not going to lose you now. Either of you. Swing Jilly this way and when the beam starts to go, push off the wall as hard as you can and grab my hand. I swear on my soul I won't let you go. Either of you.''

And then it was too late to argue. With a final groan, the air beneath her feet shifted and gravity reached up to snatch her down.

With a grunt of effort, Steph heaved her daughter toward Reid, but she didn't follow. She jammed her fingers and toes as deep as she could into the shallow cracks that seamed the old building and clung like a spider.

Reid grabbed Jilly out of midair and hustled her through the window, then shimmied back out on his meager ledge and held out a hand to her. ''Your turn, sweetheart. Trust me. I'll catch you. I love you.''

And Stephanie Alberts, who'd sworn never to put her faith in another man, let go of the wall and leapt into thin air, trusting Reid to save her.

Trusting him not to let her go.

Epilogue

"Jilly? Jilly, where are you?" The starched white lab coat flapped around Stephanie's calves as she eased up the stairs toward her daughter's bedroom. She wasn't moving so quickly these days. "Are you in here, baby?"

"I'm not your baby." Five-year-old Jilly, who hadn't stopped talking in two years, mock-scowled, though her eyes twinkled. "That's your baby." She pointed at her mother's once-flat stomach, which now resembled—at least in Stephanie's mind—the back end of a VW Beetle.

Then the child belied the complaint by pressing her face against Steph's belly and saying, "Hi, baby! When are you coming out?"

"When she's fully cooked," came the reply from above and behind Steph's shoulder, and she spun—sort of—with a glad cry and was immediately cuddled against her husband's chest. She smelled the turpentine and wondered when he'd found time to sneak upstairs to the room they'd converted to his studio.

Then she wondered if he'd finished his "surprise" yet, and she hoped that he and his brushes were kind to the curves and bumps that had developed as her pregnancy advanced. She wouldn't have posed nude for him that day, except that he'd loved her into pliant, boneless submission before arranging her on the sofa with a hot look in his eye.

Two years ago, it would have been laughable to envision tough Detective Peters as a closet oil painter. But then again, it had been almost impossible to see him as a family man. He'd turned out to be a natural at both.

"Daddy!" yelled Jilly, and immediately dove into the group hug. "You're home early!"

"It seems we both are." Reid cocked an eyebrow—a trick she was pretty sure he'd gotten Sturgeon to teach him—at Steph's lab coat. "Feeling frisky?" he whispered into Steph's ear.

It never ceased to amaze her what a starched white lab coat could do to a man. Well, to *her* man. But frankly she was feeling anything but sexy. She'd left the coat on because twisting around to take off the extra-oversized lab coat—which resembled a white pup tent—had been too much of an effort, so she'd left it on.

Her back ached, her feet hurt and she'd left work early, hoping for a nap and not expecting Reid or Jilly to be home. But Maureen and Mortimer were off on their twice-delayed honeymoon tour of jazz clubs across the country, and the babysitter had had too much homework to stay late.

"Not so much," she managed to reply, aware that Reid was looking at her strangely and that Jilly had fallen unusually silent.

"Everything okay, sweetheart?"

Though it usually warmed her when the big, bad detective who'd sworn he didn't need to be loved called her that, today it just gave her heartburn and made her backache worse.

Funny. That's about how she'd felt when she'd barely managed to drag herself out of the cab.

"Steph? What's wrong?" The first hint of concern laced Reid's voice as Stephanie began to piece one and one together and got…three.

"I don't think I'm feeling frisky, love. I think I'm feeling like having a baby."

And though they'd talked about it, planned for it, run through every contingency plan imaginable, Steph was surprised to see on her husband's face the one emotion he'd never shown her before, even when he'd been hanging out that apartment window holding onto her with just three fingers of one hand as Sturgeon and the others had struggled to pull them to safety.

Stark, abject terror.

And so, when she most needed to be soothed, she found herself soothing. When she most needed to be held, she found herself holding. When she most needed to be reassured, she found herself reassuring.

And she discovered that it was exactly what she had needed after all.

* * * * *

In April 2005, check back into Boston General Hospital for Jessica Andersen's newest medical thriller, Intensive Care, *where passion and peril reach a fever pitch.*

Coming soon from Silhouette Intrigue!

BOOK Offer Exclusive to
Silhouette Romance Series

Buy this book and get another free! Simply
indicate which series you are interested in by
ticking the box and we'll send you a FREE book.
Please tick only one box

✂

Special Edition	❏	Superromance	❏
Sensation	❏	Intrigue	❏
Desire	❏	Spotlight	❏

Please complete the following:

Name _____

Address _____

_____ Postcode _____

Please cut out and return the above coupon along with
your till receipt to:

Silhouette Free Book competition,
Reader Service
FREEPOST NAT 10298, Richmond,
Surrey TW9 1BR

▼ SILHOUETTE®
INTRIGUE™

JUST BEFORE DAWN
by Joanna Wayne

Hidden Passions: Full Moon Madness

Ever since Sara Murdoch returned to her roots to uncover the cause of her childhood nightmares, gruff neighbour Nat Sanderson sensed that danger was near. And when escalating threats prove Sara's nightmares were deadly facts, Nat could no longer deny his urge to be her protector…and lover.

ALSO AVAILABLE NEXT MONTH

VELVET ROPES by Patricia Rosemoor

SHOTGUN DADDY by Harper Allen
Bad Boys

INTENSIVE CARE by Jessica Andersen

Don't miss out! All these thrilling books are on sale from 18th March 2005

Visit our website at www.silhouette.co.uk

Available at most branches of WHSmith, Tesco, ASDA, Martins, Borders, Eason, Sainsbury's and most good paperback bookshops.

SILHOUETTE®

INTRIGUE™

proudly presents
a new series from popular author

Joanna Wayne

HIDDEN PASSIONS
Full Moon Madness

Deadly danger reveals secret desires in
the hours between dusk and dawn...

As Darkness Fell
February 2005

Just Before Dawn
April 2005

Visit our website at www.silhouette.co.uk

THE TRUEBLOOD
Dynasty

*Isabella Trueblood made history reuniting people
torn apart by war and an epidemic. Now,
generations later, Lily and Dylan Garrett carry on
her work with their agency, Finders Keepers.*

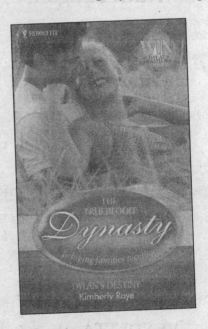

Book Twelve available from 18th February

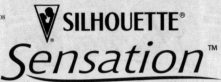

▼ SILHOUETTE®
Sensation™

is proud to present a thrilling new series
from *USA Today* bestselling author

Ruth Langan

*Beneath the surface lies scandal,
secrets...and seduction.*

COVER-UP – *March 2005*

WANTED – *April 2005*

VENDETTA – *May 2005*

RETRIBUTION – *June 2005*

Visit our website at www.silhouette.co.uk

FREE!
2 Books
and a surprise gift!

We would like to take this opportunity to thank you for reading this Silhouette® book by offering you the chance to take TWO more specially selected titles from the Intrigue™ series absolutely FREE! We're also making this offer to introduce you to the benefits of the Reader Service™—

- ★ FREE home delivery
- ★ FREE gifts and competitions
- ★ FREE monthly Newsletter
- ★ Exclusive Reader Service offers
- ★ Books available before they're in the shops

Accepting these FREE books and gift places you under no obligation to buy. you may cancel at any time. even after receiving your free shipment. Simply complete your details below and return the entire page to the address below. You don't even need a stamp!

YES! Please send me 2 free Intrigue books and a surprise gift. I understand that unless you hear from me. I will receive 4 superb new titles every month for just £3.05 each. postage and packing free. I am under no obligation to purchase any books and may cancel my subscription at any time. The free books and gift will be mine to keep in any case.

15ZEF

Ms/Mrs/Miss/Mr ....Initials.................................

BLOCK CAPITALS PLEASE

Surname ....

Address..

....Postcode ....

Send this whole page to:
UK: FREEPOST CN81, Croydon, CR9 3WZ